# TRIPLE TEST FOR TRUDY

RUTH FORBES CHANDLER

# Triple Test
# for Trudy

*illustrated by Cristina F. Christensen*

ABELARD–SCHUMAN

*London New York Toronto*

| LONDON | NEW YORK | TORONTO |
|---|---|---|
| Abelard-Schuman | Abelard-Schuman | Abelard-Schuman |
| Limited | Limited | Canada Limited |
| 8 King St. WC2 | 6 West 57th St. | 896 Queen St. W. |

Printed in the United States of America

*To The Florida Chandlers*

# CONTENTS

TRIPLE TEST FOR TRUDY

# 1: Tripps' Triangle,
## Florida

TRIPPS' TRIANGLE was one of the prettiest trailer parks in
Florida. It was small — only thirty trailers — but in the triangle were gardens, a swimming pool, a game court and
many comfortable chairs under the palms and long-
needled pines. In front was the boulevard; on the left,
Kimberly Lane. Behind the third and longest side was a
high board fence, almost hidden by flowering shrubs and
a row of punk trees. A dozen sprinklers revolved constant-
ly to keep the lawns green.

Eric Spear was glad there were sprinklers that hot October afternoon. He had skipped school for a very important and secret reason and, that matter taken care of, he
now had nothing to do, nowhere to go. As he lay under
the hibiscus behind the Warrens' trailer, waiting for his
pal, Jimmy, to come home, he rolled his dungarees higher and stretched his legs so the revolving spray would
reach them at every turn.

Eric was ten, a long, thin boy with long legs, long arms.
Even his hair was long, it hadn't been cut for two months.
He had large gray eyes, and a small tight mouth which
appeared to be zippered shut so he would not talk too
much. His ears — his sister Lorraine told him frequently —
stuck out like handles on a sugar bowl.

Hearing a car, he rolled over to see if Jimmy had come. But the car stopped at the next trailer — the Laphams. They were going to South America for the winter, Eric knew, for everybody knew everybody else's business, more or less, since they lived so close together. These must be the people to whom they were subletting their trailer.

A tall man and a slender young woman with reddish-gold hair stepped out of the car just as Mrs. Lapham appeared on the patio to ask them in.

Eric wondered if they had any children. There were very few children in the Triangle. Jimmy Warren was Eric's only real friend. When he was away there were only older boys on the grounds, and girls. Eric disliked girls, all girls, starting with his own sister whom he disliked most of all. She had locked him out of their trailer again that morning when she left for high school. He knew why. She thought she'd get home first and find his little black box before he could hide it in a different place. But she wouldn't find it. Not today. Not ever, he hoped.

He flopped over to pursue his secret thoughts halfway around the globe.

Then the Laphams' door opened. The people came out and, as usual, Eric listened.

He heard the red-haired lady's voice: "Your furnishings are lovely."

Then the man's voice: "And you needn't worry about Trudy. She's a very well-behaved child. She'll be careful of your nice things."

Eric groaned. Another girl. Another gooky girl.

Mrs. Lapham said, "The Tripps have a daughter, Nancy. She'll be delighted to have a new friend. Jimmy Warren lives there." She pointed. "He's a very nice boy. Wait a minute. I'll get my purse and ride to the office with you and introduce you to Mrs. Tripp."

Eric started to wriggle away when the woman's voice stopped him.

"Alan," she said, looking up at her husband, "would you mind terribly if we didn't send for Trudy right away?"

"Why? What do you mean?"

"I wish we could wait a few weeks until I become accustomed to living here."

"What is there to become accustomed to? She showed us where everything is."

"I know, but . . . but this is the first home we've ever had. I've loved going from place to place and living in motels, but I wish it could be just the two of us here for a little while. For one thing, I don't know much about cooking."

"Cooking? Nonsense, honey. You can cook."

"No, not really. I've never roasted a chicken or made a pie in my life. And Trudy's used to your mother's cooking, and you say she's an excellent cook."

"She is, but—"

"There's something else, Alan. I know it sounds foolish, but I'm . . . I'm scared. I want so much for Trudy to like me, but I'm not used to children. I wish that for a little while, a week or two—"

"All right, honey. It will take that long to make the arrangements. But you're worrying over nothing. You'll love Trudy and she'll love you."

"Oh, I hope so. Here's Mrs. Lapham." They got in the car and drove away.

Eric was interested. The redhead must be a stepmother and she didn't want the gooky girl to live with them. Trouble ahead! He strolled across the Triangle to the office and went in to look at the post cards and hear the rest of it.

Mrs. Tripp, the big, motherly woman who ran the trailer park, was booming out, "We'll be delighted to have her, Mr. Frost. My Nancy will be tickled pink. Is it Trudy's first visit to Florida?"

"Yes. Jean and I are planning to show her everything. She'll love it." Opening his wallet, he handed Mrs. Tripp a picture.

"What a beautiful child!" she exclaimed.

"Yes, she's a nice-looking girl. Of course she's taller now. This was taken two years ago."

"She looks like you," Mrs. Tripp said to draw Mrs. Frost into the conversation.

"Oh, no, I'm not her mother," she said quickly, her cheeks flushing. "I've never seen Trudy, but I'm looking forward to it."

"I'll bet you can hardly wait." Mrs. Tripp passed them the cards to sign.

"She won't be here for a couple of weeks because someone will have to bring her down. I'm hoping my father and mother will. Trudy has lived with them ever

since her mother died. This will be quite a change for her
— up there in Vermont she has eleven cousins, all boys.
They're the Frosts; Trudy's the Frosting. That's what
people call her."

"Frosting," Eric mumbled, "gooky Frosting." Everything he disliked was "gooky." It was his own word: he
was proud of it. And when gooky was not strong enough
he made a noise in the back of his throat, like a frog
with laryngitis. He made it now. They all turned to look
at him.

"Eric, why aren't you in school?" Mrs. Tripp demanded.

"I'm sick," he whined.

"What's the matter?"

He shrugged. "Measles, maybe."

"Eric, why do you say things like that?" Mrs. Tripp
dropped her voice and went on talking . . . about him,
Eric was sure, and his brother Barry.

He gave the post card rack a whirl that almost tipped
it over. Then, scowling, he swaggered past the Frosts and
out of the door, slamming it as hard as he could.

He crossed the grass to the nearest trailer and
scratched on the screen door with a stick until his sister
opened it. She was fifteen. She, too, had gray eyes and a
tiny mouth, but the effect was quite different, for every
day Lorraine spent hours making herself beautiful, from
the top of her stylish hairdo to her pink lacquered toe-
nails.

"Did you go to school today?" she asked.

"Nope."

"Where have you been?"

"Nowhere."

"That's a sensible answer. I saw you come out of the office. Who are the people in the Texas car?"

He shrugged without answering and looked in the refrigerator for something to eat.

"I don't suppose you'd tell me if it was the Queen of England."

"Yuh. It was. The king, too."

"Oh, you think you're so smart." She took a loaf of bread from the drawer and shoved it toward him. "You skipped school so you could hide Barry's box in a different place, didn't you? What's in it? Do you know?"

"Nope." With an utterly blank face, he hacked off a chunk of pot roast and made himself a sandwich.

# 2: *The Frost Farm,*

## *Vermont*

ONE THOUSAND FIVE HUNDRED MILES to the north, on that same October afternoon, there was a frosty nip in the air. The Vermont hills were autumn bright, although yellow leaves, already turning crisp and crackly brown, lay knee-deep under the maples. Fleecy clouds like mounds of soap bubbles sailed lazily across the bright sky.

Trudy Frost loved every season as it came. That Friday afternoon, free from school for two whole days and bursting with energy and the joy of living, she was sure that autumn was the best season of all.

As she scrambled out of school clothes and into corduroy pants and jacket, she sniffed the good smell from the kitchen where her grandmother was making piccalilli.

"Mm! It smells yummy, Gramma," she said, stopping long enough to give it a stir with the big wooden spoon.

Trudy popped a resounding kiss on her grandmother's hot pink cheek, grabbed a handful of molasses cookies from the jar that, by some miracle, was always full, and raced to the barn to saddle their pony, Pepper, and get first turn to gallop around the five-acre lot.

She had made the circuit twice before the Frost cousins began to arrive from up the hill and down the hill, and across the road.

The last two ran into the field shouting, "Gramma wants you."

"No she doesn't," Trudy yelled, cutting a corner to get away from them. A "turn" was five times around the field and she did not intend to shorten it that glorious afternoon.

As she came nearer on her next round, her oldest cousin, Jerry, made a megaphone of his hands and shouted one word, "Telephone."

Then it dawned on her that perhaps her grandmother did want her. She wheeled Pepper around. "Telephone? Honest? For me?"

"Yes, it's a call from Florida. Hurry up. Get going!"

"Florida? Goodness gracious, it may be my father." Like a streak she was gone, across the field, through the dooryard, off the pony and onto the long porch and into the kitchen.

"Was it Daddy? What did he want? Why didn't he wait to talk to me?" She looked anxiously at her plump little grandmother, knowing — without being told — that it was something important.

"You're going to be surprised," Gramma said, her cheeks pinker than before.

"Goody! I love surprises. He's coming, isn't he? When?" She grabbed her grandmother and whirled her around.

"Trudy, stop it. Stand still."

"All right." She stamped each foot solidly on the floor, plunk, plunk. "I'm standing still. Now tell me before I burst all over the place."

At that moment the door opened, and the room was

filled with boys of all sizes, from little Dicky who was
five and the tagger-on, to Jerry, who was nearly fifteen.

"It was my father," Trudy told them. "That's all I know
yet."

"Let's go into the other room so I can sit down," their
grandmother said. When they were all distributed over
the well-worn chairs and the sofa, she went on, "He
called from a motel in Tampa."

"Where's Tampa?"

"It's in Florida. He wants you to go there and spend
the winter with them."

"Wow! Did you hear that? I'm going to Florida to stay
with my father!"

"And his new wife. Don't forget her."

Trudy shot a quick glance at the photograph on the
mantelpiece. Her father had sent it in June, a picture of
him very big and handsome, and beside him a pretty
young woman who came just to his shoulder. Her hair
was beautiful, like the hair of the girls who advertise
shampoos on television. You could lift it, Trudy was sure,
and it would fall back into the same smooth, soft waves.

Her own hair, shoulder length, with wide bangs, was
straight as a string and almost as white as her grandmother's. Sometimes she wore it loose with a velvet band,
but usually in thick, stubby braids. Either way, she hated
it. She sighed deeply.

"What shall I call her?" she asked.

"Wait and see. Maybe she'll want you to call her Jean."

"I should think you'd call her mother," Dicky said.

"No, she isn't old enough to be my mother."

"How are you going to get there?" Jerry asked.

"Somebody will take me. Maybe your father. Then you can all go, too."

"Not in school time. When is Trudy going, Gramma?"

"He said in a week or two. They are in a motel now, but they've hired a trailer and you'll live in that."

"Oooo! That'll be fun."

"He wanted us to bring you down by train, but I know Grampa won't go."

"I can go alone. Put me on in Boston and Daddy'll meet me."

"Indeed you won't go alone. All the way to Florida? I'd worry myself sick every minute."

"Gramma, Gramma." Dicky kept pulling her sleeve to make her listen.

"What is it, dear?"

"You know Mrs. Hubbell? She's going to Florida. I was over at her house and she was putting things in a big suitcase."

Then all the cousins began to talk at once.

"That's right. She is."

"She's going next week."

"No, the week after."

"She's going to fly."

Trudy caught her breath. "That's the way I want to go. I want to fly. Oh, Gramma, say I can. Call her, please. Ask her if I can go when she goes."

Gramma Frost rubbed the back of her hand across her forehead. "Hold on," she begged. "You're going too fast for me. I'm not sure I want you to fly even if Minnie

Hubbell would take you. We read about such terrible accidents—"

"Oh Gramma, everybody flies. Daddy does all the time. I'm going to call her myself." Trudy rushed to the telephone.

"Trudy, wait. Florida's a big state. She may not be going anywhere near Tampa."

"Is it all right if I go over there and ask her? What harm would that do? Please, Gramma, please." She leaned over the back of her grandmother's rocking chair, arms around her neck, tipping her backwards. "Please? May I just ask her?"

"Trudy, put me down," she ordered.

"I'm strong. I wouldn't let you fall." Trudy eased the chair down gently. "May I go? May we all go?"

"Well, I suppose—" she began, but Trudy was already out of the door with a stream of cousins following her.

# 3: The Lucky Girl

THE CHILDREN FOUND Mrs. Minnie Hubbell sitting on her porch in the late afternoon sun.

"Well, well, if it isn't the Frosts and Frosting! What's going on?"

"Mrs. Hubbell—" Dicky began.

"Wait, Dicky, let me tell her," Trudy interrupted. "He says you're going to Florida. I'm going, too, to stay with my father all winter and live in a trailer. He just telephoned and asked me to come." She stopped to catch her breath. "May I go on the  plane with you?"

"Why, I guess so. Where are you going? What city?"

"Tampa. Do you know where that is?"

"Tampa? Well, I never! I'm going to St. Petersburg and my son always meets me in Tampa."

"That's perfect!" Trudy squealed. "Just think, Dicky," she said, squeezing him so hard it hurt and he struggled to get free, "I'll be way up in the sky, high as those white clouds."

"You'll be higher than that," Jerry told her. "Planes fly above the clouds. Will you go by jet?"

Mrs. Hubbell nodded. "It's a jet. Eastern Air Lines."

"Golly, I wish I could go. Perhaps my father could

25

take you to the airport. I've never seen a jet on the ground. When are you going?"

"Tuesday."

"Tuesday? You mean a week from next Tuesday," Trudy said.

"No, this coming Tuesday. My daughter is driving me to Boston. If you want to go you should make your reservation right away."

"You should ask Gramma first," Jerry warned.

"She knows I'm going, and she doesn't want me to go alone," Trudy argued.

"She said in a week or two."

"That doesn't matter if I have a way to get there. If Mrs. Hubbell is going right to Tampa—"

"I could call my travel agency and see if they have any seats left. There is always plenty of room on the midweek planes from Boston, but they fill up in New York."

New York! Trudy's heart went thumpety-thump. "Call them," she urged.

"Are you sure your grandmother wants me to?"

"Yes. That's what we came over for—to see if I could go with you."

Mrs. Hubbell put the call through while the boys stood around, their eyes as big as saucers. Trudy, alone, stood beside the window, looking up at the sky.

It was her lucky day. No doubt about it. There had been a cancellation, and a seat was available on the 5:10 plane.

"You'd better reserve it, Trudy, if you want to go,"

Mrs. Hubbell said. "Of course, your grandmother can cancel it if Tuesday is too soon."

"It isn't too soon. Tell him to save it for me. Ooo! I'm going to fly! Over the clouds, up in the sky!" She spun around the room, first on one foot, then on the other.

"You're always the lucky one," Jerry said.

"I know it. Thank you, Mrs. Hubbell. Let's go tell Gramma!"

Gramma was in the kitchen, making a pineapple up-sidedown cake for their supper.

"It's all settled," Trudy began breezily, wasting no time. "I'm flying to Tampa with Mrs. Hubbell."

"Her reservation's made," Jerry added.

"She's going to fly. Look, Gramma, way up there!" Dicky pointed to a cloud already tipped with pink from the setting sun.

"Tuesday," another cousin stated.

"Goodness gracious, don't all talk at once." She turned the heat down and beckoned to Trudy. "Now tell me. What have you done?"

Suddenly there was silence in the kitchen. Trudy looked to the boys for help, then at her grandmother, then at the floor.

"I should have waited and asked you first," she said at last. "But you say that sometimes there are decisions I should make for myself...and...and I thought this was one."

"Mrs. Hubbell offered to call the ticket office," Jerry explained. "Trudy didn't ask her to."

"And it was a long-distance call and I had to think quick." Trudy looked at her grandmother with pleading eyes. "I...I thought it was just...just everything turning out right. I can go, can't I?"

Grandmother Frost took a deep breath and went back to her butter and brown sugar. "We'll see what your grandfather says."

Trudy was worried. Grandfather would want to please her, but she was sure he would not want her to fly. She was right. He didn't. But the question of how she would get to Florida, if she didn't go with Mrs. Hubbell, remained unanswered.

"I'll sleep on it," he told her that night when she went to bed. In spite of her excitement, Trudy did sleep, which is more than her grandfather did. At breakfast he announced that since the reservation was made, and Mrs. Hubbell would look out for her, she had better go.

"But Tuesday!" her grandmother wailed. "I can't get her ready by Tuesday. She'll need new clothes—"

"Daddy'll buy me clothes when I get there," Trudy argued.

"I don't want his new wife to think I've neglected you—"

"Gramma, you haven't." Trudy held out her plate for more griddle cakes and bacon. "You've given me everything I ever wanted."

"Your father said in a week or two. They aren't in the trailer yet."

"I don't mind living in a motel. I'd like it. I bet my father wants me to come as soon as I can."

"She's right about that," her grandfather agreed.

Gramma Frost gave a troubled sigh. "Well, I'll wash today and make a list of the things you'll need. Monday we'll go shopping. What time does your plane leave?"

"Ten minutes past five."

"Ten minutes past five? At night? Oh, I don't like that. You'll be flying in the dark."

"What of it? Lots of planes fly at night. May I call Daddy and tell him I'm coming?"

"No." Her grandfather stacked his dishes and carried them to the sink. "We'll call him tonight when the rates are lower."

The day flew by. There were friends to astound with the good news. There were the usual chores to be done, the baby Frost cousins to care for, as well as games and extra rides on the pony. Every single thing was special that Saturday because it would not be done again for a long, long time.

At nine o'clock Trudy's grandfather dialled the long-distance operator and gave the number his son had asked him to call.

Too excited to keep still, Trudy danced around the room, ran to the kitchen for a drink of water, then hurried back, for her father was on the line. He was surprised that she was coming so soon, but they'd be at the airport to meet her.

"Are there any children in the trailer park?" Trudy asked.

"Yes. I met a girl named Nancy this morning."

"Any boys?"

"There's a bright-looking boy named Jimmy in the next trailer, and there's one named Eric. That's all I've seen so far."

"I've never known anybody named Eric. Oh, Daddy, I'm so happy I can hardly wait!"

"And I can hardly wait to see my little girl."

"Big girl," she corrected. "I'm almost as tall as Jerry." She turned the phone over to her grandmother for a last good-bye.

Sunday was church and Sunday school. By that afternoon everybody in the little village of Pottersville knew that Trudy Frost was going to fly to Florida to spend the winter with her father and his new wife.

Monday morning Grampa drove them to town to do their shopping.

In one store Trudy saw a beautiful dress—a sleeveless pink taffeta with roses on it. It had a round low neck and a crisp full skirt. She stopped, unable to pass it by.

"Gramma, I ought to have a party dress," she said.

"That's too old for you. Come on."

A smiling saleswoman came nearer. "I think it's just her size. Would you like to try it on?"

"May I, Gramma? Just to see how I'd look?"

"No, there isn't enough time. We haven't bought your socks and shoes yet, and your grandfather wants to get home by twelve o'clock."

"I'll take my old ones. They don't matter. But I need a party dress." She smiled at the saleswoman. "You see, I'm going to Florida. Tomorrow!" It came out with a gasp, almost too wonderful to be true.

Trudy tried on the pink dress. It turned her into a dazzling pink butterfly.

"Oh, you should take it," the saleswoman raved. "It's exactly right for your school dances." She saw the disapproving look in Gramma's eye and added, "It's what all the teen-agers are wearing."

"Trudy's only eleven years old."

"But I'll be twelve next month." As she looked at her reflection in the triple mirror, at the dress and at herself, Trudy realized for the first time that it was going to be terribly exciting to grow up and wear pretty clothes. She smoothed her bangs and pushed her hair back behind her ears. "I look like a teen-ager, don't I?"

"Nonsense," her grandmother snapped. "You're only a little girl. Take that off and put on your own dress."

"Gramma, I really need it. You could call it my Christmas present."

"No."

"It was lovely on her," the saleswoman said sadly as she put the dress back on the rack.

Trudy made one more try.

"If somebody should invite me to a party, shall I wear the blue gingham you just bought or my old white dress that you had to let the hem out of?"

Her grandmother hesitated. The next minute Trudy was hugging her so hard she could hardly breathe, and that was it.

By the time they returned to the car, loaded with bundles, the precious dress in the big blue box under Trudy's arm, her grandfather could see that she was—as he put it

—high as a kite, and his poor wife was worn to a frazzle.

The whole family came to supper that night: three aunts, three uncles, and eleven cousins, including the babies. The aunts brought enough food for an army.

For dessert there was ice cream and a big cake with a toy airplane on top, and a tiny yellow-haired doll. It was a real party. Afterwards, the aunts excused Trudy from helping with the dishes so she and Gramma played with the babies.

When all the work was done, they talked about Florida, although none of them had ever been there, and about planes, although none of them had ever flown. The aunts wanted to see the new pink dress. Trudy put it on and whirled on tiptoe, bowing and dancing, her eyes like stars, her cheeks as red as roses.

"There's no doubt about it," Dicky's father said admiringly, "she's the Family Frosting!"

When they went home, Trudy kissed them all, promising to write and tell them everything she did, or saw, or heard.

When the house was quiet again, she was ready to go to bed. But for a long time she lay awake, her mind a jumble of Frosts, and party dresses, and airplanes flying high, high, higher than the clouds in the moonlit sky.

# 4: The Big Day

THE MORNING OF THE BIG DAY dawned dark and drizzly. Trudy was up early.

After breakfast she made one last trip to the barn to say good-bye to the pony, the dog, the old grandmother cat and as many of her descendants as she could find. Then she dressed in her going-away clothes, and her grandfather drove her to the little school at the four corners.

Trudy knew every inch of that school. She knew both teachers and every one of the fifty-nine children. As she tiptoed up the stairs, she could hear her cousin Robert explaining an arithmetic problem. It was exciting to be a visitor, stopping in for a minute.

Her cards were ready, but the teacher asked Trudy to stay while the children found Tampa on the map.

They all liked her; they were glad for her, but their good-byes were tinged with just a touch of envy. She was always the lucky one. She knew it and walked on air as she lingered in the downstairs room to make the delightful business of saying farewell last as long as possible.

Her grandmother was still packing when she got home. "Everything's there now," she said, "underwear, blouses, shorts, skirts, dresses." She ticked them off on her fingers while Trudy stood gloating over the pink taffeta that billowed up between layers of tissue paper.

She closed the bag, locked it, and gave Trudy the key. "Put it in your handbag. Don't lose it, and keep your eye on the suitcase. Your grandfather paid for your ticket and here's five dollars for you. It should take care of everything."

"Thanks." Trudy put the bills into her billfold, zippered the pocket of her handbag and snapped it shut.

"Sit down a minute." Gramma Frost stared out of the window, trying to put her thoughts into words. "Your father is very happy now," she said at last. "He deserves to be happy. Be sure you never do anything to make him unhappy, or Jean, either."

"I won't," Trudy promised. "I won't be any trouble."

"You wouldn't mean to be. But it's going to be hard for Jean to have a big girl... like you... the child of another marriage... come to live with her so soon. Be nice to her. Remember what I say. Be a good girl."

"Yes. Of course I will."

Trudy sat at the window for nearly an hour, waiting for the Hubbells to arrive. Then came the last good-bye. Gramma and Grampa waved, turned and went back into the house. There were no tears. They would miss her terribly, Trudy knew, but they were not the crying kind.

She had an ache in her throat, though, that kept her from talking for the first few miles. But she was headed

for Boston, for New York, for Florida! She didn't feel
sad very long.

For hours they drove along the rain-soaked highways
to Logan Airport and Eastern Airlines Terminal, where
Mrs. Hubbell's daughter left them and started her long
ride home.

A porter took their bags and they followed him into
the waiting room where he laid them on a counter. A
man weighed them and, to Trudy's consternation, set
them on a moving belt which carried them off out of
sight.

"I want to keep my bag with me," she protested.

The man handed her a baggage check. "Don't worry,"
he said. "When you get to Tampa it'll be there waiting
for you."

"I hope so." She put the check in her handbag with the
key and the five dollars.

"Now," Mrs. Hubbell said, "we'll go and see if our
plane is in."

It was a long walk past many waiting rooms to the
end of the building. Outside was a huge red-white-and-
blue plane with an American flag and the name *Golden
Falcon* painted on its side. Each of the long, broad wings
had two jet engines under it.

"Oh, wouldn't Jerry love to see this!" Trudy exclaimed.

They waited to show their tickets, and walked through
the drizzle, up the steps. At the door a pretty stewardess
welcomed them as they came aboard.

Trudy stepped inside. Soft music was playing, and
lights in a glowing pattern shone through the gold trim

above the narrow windows. The seats, three on each side of the aisle, were upholstered in gold and blue fabric. The overhead racks held people's coats, and small, white pillows.

"Trudy, sit here," Mrs. Hubbell said, "the farther back we sit, the more you can see. If you're over the wing you can't see anything."

Trudy sank down into a high-backed seat next to the window.

"It's so big!" she said. "I thought the inside of a plane would be more like a bus." She looked at her watch. Ten minutes to five. Twenty minutes to wait! She watched a motor truck with baggage unloading at the front end of the plane. People were boarding there, too. Her stomach churned like an electric egg beater, matching the rhythm of the motors which at first she had hardly noticed, but which now grew louder.

After a while a small sign lit up on the back of the seat in front of her: NO SMOKING. FASTEN YOUR SEAT BELTS. A stewardess walked down the aisle to make sure everyone obeyed the signs.

"Is this your first flight?" she asked Trudy.

"Yes. Isn't it almost time we started?"

"In a few minutes."

When they did start, the plane taxied on the ground, up one runway and down another. Then they waited while several planes, which were ahead of them, took off. At last the *Falcon's* engines began to roar. Down the long straight runway it raced, faster and faster, its broad wings almost touching the ground. Trudy could not tell the exact minute they were airborne, but now they were up and there was the city down below, and a green park, and the waters of the bay.

Almost immediately everything disappeared and there was nothing to see but fog and thick gray mist. She felt uneasy, remembering how her grandfather hated to drive on foggy nights. Apparently here everything was all right, for the Fasten-your-seat-belts sign went off, the stewardess was smiling, and the Captain's voice came over the loudspeaker, telling them they would fly at an altitude of 16,000 feet and would arrive in New York in fifty-five minutes.

Fascinated, Trudy watched the hinged plates on the wings open and close, and open again. Everything was quiet; there was no more music, and almost no vibration from the powerful motors. She had a strange feeling of not moving, of simply hanging in the air.

In a few minutes the stewardess brought hot coffee and a coke which she placed on little trays that pulled down from the seats in front.

"Don't we have to pay?" Trudy whispered.

"No, not for our dinner, either," Mrs. Hubbell assured her.

"Goodness! Aren't airplanes wonderful!"

Before she finished her coke, the light changed. Trudy looked out of the window, and gasped. The sun was shining in the bluest of skies. Down below was...what? Could it be snow? Miles and miles and miles of the purest, whitest snow—that's what it looked like—with breaks near

the horizon, dazzling blue, exactly like blue water showing through drifting ice.

"Look, Mrs. Hubbell! Is it snow?" she asked.

"Those are the clouds we came through."

Trudy felt a prickle of delight run through her body.
This was lovelier than anything she had ever imagined.
As she watched, a shimmering rainbow—elliptical in
shape—appeared above the cloud bank. Far back on her
left, a full moon shone pale against the vivid blue of the
sky.

"It's so beautiful," she said softly, "so very beautiful."

Then the lights came on, reminding them to fasten
their seat belts. They were approaching New York.

"Already? It doesn't seem possible!" There was a roar-
ing in her ears and she swallowed to get rid of it as they
went into the fog again. When she could see the ground
below, it was the outline of the shore with small houses
along the edge, then roads, and groups of buildings, and
more houses laid out in perfect squares—miles and miles
of houses.

Suddenly the plane banked and the houses, instead of
being down below, rose way up to the top of the window, where the sky ought to be.

"Did you see that?" Trudy asked.

"We're turning. We're almost there."

Then they seemed to go faster and faster and lower
and lower, and her ears buzzed uncomfortably as they
roared past stretches of scraggly grass and onto the runway of New York's Kennedy Airport.

The airfield was still wet, but the rain had stopped. They left cards saying OCCUPIED in their seats, took tickets from the stewardess to be admitted back on the plane, and went for a walk.

Looking around, hoping to catch sight of at least one skyscraper, Trudy noticed a long line of people moving steadily toward their plane.

"Don't you think we'd better go back?" she said, and Mrs. Hubbell agreed.

As they boarded the plane, the stewardess asked them if they were enjoying the trip.

Trudy assured her they were. "Why do some people go in the front door? she asked.

"That is the First Class section. Would you like to see it?"

Trudy followed the stewardess, and Mrs. Hubbell followed Trudy because she had never seen a First Class section either.

There were two seats on each side of the aisle, instead of three, so that the passengers had more room. They had footstools, too.

"And their food is different," the stewardess said.

"Do you cook meals on the plane?" Trudy asked, wondering how the three girls could manage, knowing that it took a dozen women all afternoon to get ready for a church supper.

"The food comes on board here at the Kennedy Airport, piping hot, in trays." She showed them the tiny kitchen— the ovens with warming racks, the coffee urns, and the refrigerator.

Then she let them peep into the nose of the plane. It

was an unbelievably small place. Every inch of wall space
was covered with gadgets and lights, hundreds of them.
There were buttons and dials and gauges on the left, on
the right, and even overhead. The two pilots' seats were
empty, but near them, at a table covered with diagrams
and maps, another man was still working.

"How do you like flying?" he asked.

"I love it."

"Good! That's what we like to hear."

They went back to their seats. Waiting was interesting
because lights were shining everywhere—red, blue,
green, lemon yellow and gold. More people boarded until every seat was taken.

The seat belt signs flashed on again, there was more
taxiing and waiting, and then the roar of the take-off.
The Captain announced that they would fly at an altitude
of 31,000 feet and reach Tampa in two hours and forty
minutes.

Trudy sighed with complete happiness as she watched
the moon turn more golden while, through the windows
on the opposite side, she could see a glorious pink and
gold sunset. It would certainly take a long, long letter
to tell the folks back home about this wonderful day!

Before the sunset faded the stewardess brought dinner;
roast lamb, vegetables, salad, dessert, each in a small
container that fitted into the plastic tray so that nothing
would slide or spill. It was a delicious meal.

By the time they finished, the sky was full of stars,
but down below, they saw only darkness. It was impos-
sible to realize that they were almost six miles above the
earth, flying at tremendous speed.

# 5: *On to Florida*

In New York a woman had taken the seat beside Mrs. Hubbell and now they were talking together. Trudy amused herself by going through the pocket of the seat in front. There was an enormous map with hundreds of red lines, each indicating an air route. She found Vermont, New York, and Tampa, remembering how her class had done it that morning. It seemed a week ago!

Then she pulled out a paper bag. "What's this for?" she asked.

"Put it back," Mrs. Hubbell told her. "It's to use if you're sick."

Trudy put it back fast and pulled out a card, giving instructions in English on one side, and in Spanish on the other, about what to do if they crashed into the sea.

She read for a while but her thoughts kept flying ahead to Tampa, to her father and Jean.

She suddenly realized that she didn't know her father very well. His work as a citrus fruit specialist took him all over the south and southwest to talk to orange growers about soil analysis and the use of new chemical fertilizers which his company sold. She had heard him tell Grampa and her uncles about it, and she was very proud of him.

To her he was a kind of perpetual Santa Claus, coming

43

oftener, staying longer, always loaded with gifts for all the family, but spending most of his time with her.

She loved him. She loved him very much, not the way she loved Gramma and Grampa with an everyday, take-it-for-granted love, but with a sort of holiday, very special love. Would he get cross sometimes, put his foot down and say No? Would he take care of her if she cut her finger or got sick from eating too much?

Or would Jean do it? She was too young and pretty to be like the stepmothers in fairy tales, but she might be bossy. She might not like having—what was it Gramma said?—the child of another marriage to take care of.

Trudy sighed. Memories of her own mother had grown dim during the happy years on the farm, but she knew deep down in her heart that she had missed something precious. Gramma was not really like a mother. She was too old, almost sixty. Daddy was thirty-five; Jean, twenty-seven. She had been a secretary to one of the vice-presidents in the Texas office, Daddy had written, but she came from Denver, Colorado. Texas, Colorado, Florida! Faraway places. Trudy said the names over and over to herself.

The children. What would they be like? Would Nancy be fun, or would she want to sew and things like that? Trudy liked boys better because they did more interesting things.

Jimmy. She knew two boys named Jimmy—Jimmy Plaisted, who was fat and stupid, and her cousin Jimmy, who put snow down her neck in winter and grasshoppers in summer...at least he tried to. She hoped the Florida Jimmy was not like either of them.

Eric. She pictured him as tall and dark like Jerry, in junior high. He'd be the one to invite her to the dance. She'd wear the pink dress and a pink velvet band on her hair.

The Captain's voice roused her from her reverie. "The lights you see below," he said, "are in Columbia, South Carolina."

"Oh." Trudy watched for lights of highways and towns during the remaining hour, her excitement growing as they circled in lower and lower over a land of twinkling lights—millions of lights, it seemed, spread out over a million miles of roads and bridges, peninsulas and islands, all sparkling like Christmas trees hung with diamonds and sapphires, rubies and emeralds.

For another minute her ears buzzed; then with a little bump the plane landed. She opened her handbag to make sure she had not lost the baggage check, said good-bye to the stewardess, hurried down the steps into the terminal building, through the gates, and into her father's arms.

"Trudy, darling," he said, kissing her. Then he turned to Jean. "Here she is, honey. Here's our little girl."

Jean held out her arms and Trudy kissed her. Her first impression was of delicate fragrance and beautiful hair, more red than gold, and every bit as soft and shining as Trudy had imagined. While the Hubbells were saying good-bye she noticed other things. Jean's eyes were brown; she had a dimple in her cheek. She wore a gray, sleeveless dress, and spike-heeled pumps, but no stockings.

"Did you have a good flight?" she asked.

"Yes." They stood smiling at each other, not quite knowing what to say next.

"Come on, we'll get your bag," Mr. Frost said, and they went to pick up her precious suitcase as it came whirling down a moving belt onto a wide metal shelf.

"Now we'll call Gramma and tell her you arrived safe and sound."

It was strange to be on the Florida end of the line, with her grandparents' voices coming from so far away.

"Be a good girl," her grandmother said.

"Oh, Gramma, I couldn't be anything else! I like her. She's awfully pretty. Yes. I promise. I won't get into trouble. I'll be good."

They walked past hundreds of cars to find her father's blue station wagon. "You won't need this for a while," he said, tossing Trudy's winter coat onto the back seat. "It was over eighty degrees here this noon."

"It was only thirty-seven at home. We've had frost twice."

With Trudy between them on the wide front seat, they drove for miles past brightly lighted stores and motels, and Trudy saw palm trees for the first time. Leaving the city, they drove on through suburbs and over a bridge, then out into the country to Tripps' Triangle, and the air-conditioned trailer that was to be her home.

Trudy had never seen anything as luxurious in Vermont. They entered by a small tiled patio, furnished with a dainty white iron sofa and chairs, brightly cushioned, and small glass-topped tables. The living room had wall-to-wall carpeting; the kitchen was yellow, and there were two bedrooms with a connecting bathroom.

Trudy's father carried her bag to the farther room. Everything was lavender—spread, curtains, rugs, and the shades on the crystal lamps. He smiled as he slid back the door of a large closet.

"How do you like it?" he asked.

"It's beautiful. It's like Hollywood and the movies!"

Jean smiled. "Do you want us to help you unpack?"

"I can do it. But first I want to show you my party dress."

Her father unlocked the suitcase and flipped up the clasps and Trudy took the pink dress from its wrappings.

"You'll look like a million dollars," he said as she held it under her chin.

"I call it my Christmas present. Gramma didn't really want to buy it."

"It's. . . it's very pretty," Jean said.

"Don't you like it?" Trudy asked.

"Of course. It's just that the children here live in bathing suits and play clothes. But maybe there'll be parties."

"My birthday's in November. I could have a party."

"The trailer's pretty small for parties, but we can go to some nice place for dinner that night so you can wear it."

"That'll be fun."

The unpacking did not take long. When Jean stepped out to set the table, Trudy whispered, "Daddy, what shall I call her?"

"You can call her Mummy."

"She isn't old enough to be my mother."

"Call me Jean," she said, appearing in the doorway. "And now come and have a cool drink and some cookies."

For a long time they sat at the dinette table, talking. There was so much to tell about the family and the changes in town.

"Bored to death, Jean?" her husband asked.

"No. I'm getting acquainted with the multitudinous Frosts. I hope to meet them all some day."

"You will. We wanted to come home last spring, but Jean had to work almost to the day we were married. Then I was sent to California and we were there until mid-September. We'll make it next summer, though, maybe sooner. Won't we, Jean?"

"Daddy, may I stay until then and go back when you do? I'd love that."

"We'll see when the time comes. Right now you should be in bed. It's ten o'clock, eleven by your time."

It was strange to kiss them goodnight and go off by herself to the little room at the back of the trailer. It was strange to remove the spread and find only sheets, and the blanket folded on a chair. It was strange to turn off the light and get into the little low bed, while soft music from the Hi-Fi in the living room mingled with the sound of her father's voice and Jean's low laughter.

It was so strange that for a minute she felt terribly lonely. But only for a minute. It had been a big day. She was tired, very tired, and she was soon asleep.

# 6: *The Triangle Children*

THE NEXT FEW DAYS were busy ones. Alan Frost had planned his work so that he could spend as much time as possible with Trudy. First he took her for a walk around the Triangle, telling her the names of the strange plants and showing her an orange tree with hard, dark green oranges almost hidden among the shiny leaves.

Each trailer had its own tiny flower garden or carefully tended window box, bright awnings and outdoor tables and chairs. The number plates on the cars were from Oregon, Maine, Oklahoma, Massachusetts and a dozen other states, but the trailer homes had taken root in the sandy Florida soil and looked as though they never intended to move again.

Trudy sniffed the cool, sweet air, trying to find the mockingbird and red birds that sang above her head. "Oh, Daddy, it's so beautiful! I'd like to stay here forever!"`

"I thought you'd like it. Come on to the office. I want to introduce you to Mrs. Tripp."

Mrs. Tripp hugged Trudy and promised that Nancy would be over right after school. Mr. Tripp, a thin, tired-looking man, left his lawn mower and came over to shake hands.

After a few minutes Mr. Frost said, "If we're going to Silver Springs, we'd better get started."

That's the kind of day it was, one thrill after another.

They rode through miles of orange groves and on past ranch lands where enormous Brahman cattle were grazing and the herdsmen wore cowboy hats. Then on to Silver Springs for a ride in a glass-bottomed boat. Trudy was breathless with wonder at the underwater fairyland, the strange formations of ledge and rock and cavern, and the tame fish. She bought a dozen post cards to send home, but how could she make her grandparents and cousins understand what it was really like?

And only yesterday at this time she had been riding through the cold rain to Boston! It didn't seem possible.

The next day was even more exciting, for they went to Cypress Gardens to see the water skiing. Trudy had seen that on television, but to have the races, the high jumps and the kiteflight take place before her eyes was a hundred times more thrilling.

Again that night they had dinner in a cool, dark restaurant and stayed there a long time, driving home by moonlight. Oh my, Trudy thought, Vermont was never like this!

On Friday Mr. Frost had to work, so Jean suggested that she and Trudy spend the day at St. Petersburg Beach with a friend of hers. Trudy was delighted. Since she had no swimsuit, they stopped to buy one.

"Here's a pretty one!" Trudy pointed to a pink nylon stretch on one of the display models.

"That's too old for you." Jean picked up a crinkle-knit

with narrow yellow and orange stripes. "How about this? It has a lot of style."

"I'd feel like a caterpillar. I want the other one."

"But it's not suitable, dear. You haven't the figure for it."

"I know what I like."

Blue eyes met brown for a long, uncomfortable minute while Trudy sized up Jean as she would a substitute teacher, to see how far she dared to go. But Jean wasn't a new teacher. She was a permanent stepmother. Trudy decided it might be wise to take the crinkle-knit, but the incident left her with an unhappy, dissatisfied feeling that lasted the rest of the morning.

She had talked so much on the previous days that she could think of nothing to say as they drove down the scenic highway. Jean was quiet, too.

They reached the friend's house in time for luncheon, and then went to the beach. It was lovely. Palm trees lined the avenue. The sand, clean, white and hot, stretched as far as she could see. And the unbelievably warm water was the Gulf of Mexico!

Back at the house, as she showered and dressed, Trudy knew that she had stayed in the sun too long. Her shoulders and back were scarlet. When Jean's friend served tall glasses of chilled fruit juice, Trudy drank three and was still thirsty.

Upon returning to Tampa they went to her father's office. He introduced them to his secretary, and showed Trudy the big safe, and richly furnished rooms.

"Let's drive up the coast for dinner and get cooled off. I've had a tough day," he said, putting an arm around each of his two girls and steering them toward the elevator.

It was all so different from Vermont! Grampa liked his meals on time: breakfast at seven; dinner at twelve; supper at six. "While the clock is striking," Gramma said. Here they ate any old time. The food was so different, too. Trudy loved the restaurants—the music, soft lights, big menus, pretty waitresses hovering around. She loved choosing what to eat. But that night she was hot and tired. She ordered stuffed shrimp because her father did, and ice cream with marshmallow, caramel and nuts. It was good. She ate it all.

By the time they reached home, she wished she hadn't. Her stomach felt awful, her sunburn hurt, her head ached. She sat on the sofa and closed her eyes, hoping that if she kept perfectly still the horrible feeling would go away.

"What's the matter?" her father asked. "Don't you feel well?"

"No. I...I think I'm going to be sick."

Jean jumped up. "Go into the bathroom. Don't be sick on the carpet. Look, Alan, she's positively green!"

Trudy got to the bathroom in time, and she was sick, terribly sick. When it was over she felt like a wet dishcloth, wrung out. Her father and Jean helped her undress. Exhausted, she fell asleep at once and slept until nine the next morning.

She woke feeling fine and hungry.

"Take it easy for a while," her father said. "This afternoon we'll take just a short ride. We don't want to tire you out before school begins." He and Jean left to go shopping, and Trudy stayed on the patio to finish the letter to her grandmother and watch for Nancy, Jimmy and Eric, and the other Triangle children.

It was just as well that she could not see Eric at that moment. Dressed in bathing trunks and a jersey, he was mopping the linoleum. He did it exactly the way he mowed grass, pushing as hard as he could until he hit something.

Lorraine sat on the step, carefully changing her nail polish from shell pink to carmine. When Eric came out to squeeze the mop, she said, "We'll probably see the new girl today. Mrs. Tripp says she's a cute little thing."

"She isn't little. She's tall and skinny."

"Oh, so you've seen her." A crafty smile flitted across Lorraine's face. "So that's where you were last night! And you say you don't like girls!"

"I was coming out of Jimmy's. We both saw her. So what?" He scowled, knowing she'd tricked him into telling. He had watched, not because he cared a hoot about the gooky girl, but because he was interested in the stepmother business.

"Are you going to the pool?"

"I guess so."

"Eric, where's Mom's necklace?"

"I don't know." Lorraine's habit of jumping from one subject to another always annoyed him. She was like a grasshopper, jumping from a flower to a chair to a boy's shirt for no reason at all. He could never keep up with her.

"I'll give you a dollar if you'll show me what's in Barry's box."

"Nothing doing."

"Mom was crying again last night. Didn't you hear her?"

"Nope." He rinsed the mop and squeezed it again.

"It's your fault. You know where Barry is. You know where the necklace is. Which one of you found it? Was it Barry, or was it you?" She grabbed his shoulder and pulled him around, but he pushed the mop hard against her legs.

"You'll be sorry," she said, stepping back.

Eric laid the mop in the sun to dry. He was already sorry. His secret was too big for a ten-year-old boy to carry alone. He wished Barry would come back and take care of the box himself. It worried Eric day and night.

Turning quickly, he almost bumped into Rodney Davis—a big, square-headed fellow who liked Lorraine, which explained why he was going to the pool with the younger children. Lorraine had to go because she took care of the little Colton girls, Polly and Pam.

Eric tagged along after them as Nancy Tripp and her friend, mousy Maida Verazzi, came running across the grass.

"We'll get Jimmy, and then I'm going to ask the new girl to go to the pool with us," Nancy said.

"Eric's been staying out nights, watching for her to come home," Lorraine told them.

"I have not," he growled, turning scarlet to his ears.

"Lorraine, you're mean to tease him all the time," Nancy said.

"He likes it."

Jimmy came out then, and they all walked over to Trudy's.

"Welcome to Tripps' Triangle," Nancy said, tossing her long brown bob back over her shoulders. "I'm Nancy. These are the Trianglers — Jimmy, Pam, Polly, Maida, Lorraine, Eric, Rodney. We all know that you're Trudy Frost. Would you like to go to the pool with us?"

"Yes." Trudy couldn't match names and faces, but she smiled at them all.

"Are you Frosty the Snow Man?" three-year-old Polly asked.

"Not Frosty. Frost," Trudy explained.

"Hey, what's Frost doing in Florida?" Eric asked, to prove he cared nothing about this gooky girl. "Start the smudge fires! Pick the oranges!"

"Eric, stop," Nancy begged.

"Eric? You're . . . you're Eric?" Trudy stared at him, hoping she had heard wrong.

"Eric? Yes, I'm Eric," he mocked, flushing again as he saw the shocked expression on her face. "And you're Frosting."

Trudy's eyes opened wider. "How did you know that?"

He shrugged. "I just knew it. Vanilla Frosting."

"Dry up," Rodney ordered, grabbing Eric and holding a hand over his mouth. "You're from Vermont, Trudy?"

"Yes, I flew down on a big jet—"

"Alone?" Lorraine asked.

"No, with a lady. We saw—"

"I flew from California to New York alone when I was only nine."

"On a super-jet and it blew up," Eric shrieked.

Rodney grabbed him more firmly. "Stop showing off. Go on, Lorraine. Tell her about it. I'll keep this insect quiet."

"There's not much to tell. Something went wrong with the fuel line and the oil was heating, but we couldn't land with a full load so we went out over the ocean and dumped four thousand gallons."

"Wow!" Trudy was impressed.

"When we did land, they had emergency crew all over the field to put out the fires if we crashed. That's all."

Trudy could see that her flight was pretty tame compared to Lorraine's. She changed the subject to Vermont, hoping to impress them as she told about her home state. But these amazing children were not impressed. They seemed to know everything already.

Rodney had been skiing in Vermont; Maida had lived in Paris. Jimmy's father was a chauffeur for a rich man who summered in Maine. Mr. Colton was a chef at a college in Lakeland, and every June the family flew north to his summer job in Connecticut. Eric and Lorraine were from New Jersey; Nancy's people came from New York.

All the children wanted to talk about themselves. There was nothing for Trudy to do but listen.

"Well, are we going to the pool or are we going to stay here all morning?" Lorraine asked.

"You go along. I'll wait for Trudy to change," Nancy said.

As he passed behind Trudy, Eric gave one of her braids a good hard yank. Why he did it, he did not know. Perhaps he was showing off. Perhaps he liked the gooky

hair on this gooky girl. Anyway, he pulled the braid and gave her sunburned shoulder a shove.

Instantly his wrist was caught in a grip of iron. He was twisted around and looking into the bluest, angriest eyes he had ever seen. He struggled to get free, but there was no getting away from Trudy Frost when she made up her mind to hold on. He pulled harder. Over went the glass-topped table with a crash.

"Now see what you've done. My . . . my mother will be furious." She gave him a push that sent him sprawling.

"She isn't your mother. She's your stepmother. And she didn't want you to come," he yelled, rubbing his wrist.

"I don't believe it."

"Ask her, Frosting." He made his horrid throaty noise and started for the pool.

"Don't mind what he says. You know it isn't true," Nancy said. "Lorraine was telling everybody he likes you and it made him mad. But he does like you. I can tell. He's a funny boy."

"I don't see anything funny about him."

"He is rude sometimes. His mother can't control him. She works in a restaurant. His father's in Germany, in the Army."

Trudy wasn't listening. "I don't think I'll go to the pool today," she said.

"That's all right. You can go there any time. How long are you staying?"

"All winter."

"Then you'll be going to school here. When do you start?"

"Monday."

"What grade?"

"Sixth."

"I'm in seventh grade, on the Junior High side, but it's all the same building. We have over a thousand pupils. I'll stop for you Monday morning."

"My father will take me the first day."

"Why bother him? I take in all the new Triangle children. How long are you staying?"

"I'm going back in the spring." Suddenly she wished it were sooner, next month, next week, and that she didn't have to go to the new school at all.

Nancy studied Trudy's face, trying to read her thoughts. "There are three sixth grades, you know."

No, Trudy didn't know. She wished Nancy would go away, but Nancy loved to talk.

Most of their families, she said, were permanents who left their trailers in the Triangle year after year. Some day her father hoped to make the park larger, but the woman who owned the adjoining land refused to sell. She had put up the high board fence. Nancy's father had planted the punk trees to hide it.

She broke off some blossoms to show Trudy, little white flowerets around a central stem, like miniature bottle brushes.

"They look like the Clethra in our meadow," Trudy said. Our meadow! She could almost smell it, and see it, and the rocky hillside beyond. She could almost hear the tinkle of Buttercup's bell as she led the other cows to the gate at milking time.

"Here come your father and mother," Nancy said.

"Daddy, the table broke." Trudy's eyes filled with sudden tears.

"It wasn't her fault," Nancy stated loyally, as Jean tried to fit the pieces together. "Eric tipped it over."

"Don't cry. I'll mend it," Mr. Frost said. "When we leave, we'll buy them a new one. It's nothing to get upset about."

"I guess I'll go along," Nancy said. "See you Monday morning."

Trudy put her letter back in the box. She couldn't finish it. A post card would have to do again today.

"Would you like to ask Nancy to go with us this afternoon?" Jean asked.

"No."

"Do you feel all right? You're not going to be sick again?"

"No, you needn't worry."

It was not the words as much as the tone of voice that made Jean ask, "Trudy, is anything wrong?"

She didn't answer because she didn't know the answer. She must remember the exact words that hateful boy had spoken and think about them; because if they were true, something was wrong. Terribly, terribly wrong.

# 7: *Homesick or Something*

TRUDY WAS QUIET DURING LUNCH. Even when they were speeding along the broad highway, she had little to say. She sighed a tremendous sigh. She was so unhappy. Jean was partly the cause, but it was more than Jean. It was Eric and Nancy. It was the big school, and being so far from Gramma and Grampa. She sighed again.

"I thought you were asleep," her father said. "You haven't peeped for fifty miles."

"I haven't been asleep. Where did you say we're going?"

"To see the Raymonds. They used to live in Vermont, but they fell in love with Florida and bought a house and a small orange grove and settled here for good."

"Would you like it if we did that?" Jean asked.

"No. I like Vermont better." Trudy looked at the never-ending palmettos, the dead trees hung with dreary gray moss. It was strange she had not noticed them before. Vermont was much prettier with its meadows of golden-rod and asters, its hayfields and apple trees, hills and lakes and fast-running brooks.

"You'll like the Raymonds," her father said.

Trudy did like them and their house, their garden, and

their Flower House, a kind of potting shed covered with bougainvillea vines. They had kittens, too, scary little things, but Trudy caught one, then another, and stayed outdoors all afternoon watching them play.

When the grownups came out again, the kittens disappeared under the house.

"Oh," Trudy wailed. "I wish they hadn't run away. They were so cute."

"Don't you want one?" Mr. Raymond asked.

"Daddy, may I have the gray one with white paws? He likes me."

"How do you know? Did he tell you so?" her father teased.

"He purred it to me. Please, Daddy. I want him so very much."

"All right, if you want him."

At the same second Jean said, "No. Oh, Alan, no."

Trudy looked at her, closed her lips tightly, and walked away.

Mr. Raymond broke the awkward silence. "My son sent us a bushel of McIntosh apples. Come on Alan. I'll get you some."

Mrs. Raymond took her cutting shears. "And I'll pick some flowers for you." She passed them to Jean, then walked behind her to the house, hand in hand with Trudy.

"Don't sulk," she whispered, sounding so much like Gramma Frost that Trudy had to smile.

As they were leaving Mr. Raymond said, "Let me know

if you change your minds about the kitten. We've got to get rid of them. I always hate to do it."

Jean put her arm around Trudy's shoulder as they drove away. "I'm sorry you're disappointed, dear," she said. "Baby kittens are darling. I love them, too. But a trailer park is no place for a pet. And we must think of the Laphams' furnishings. Kittens scratch carpets and get hairs all over everything, and they climb on curtains and get on the beds—"

"Could one small kitten do all those terrible things?" her husband asked.

"He could." Jean's voice was firm. "And have fleas, too."

"I thought he'd be company for Trudy until she makes a few friends—"

"Nancy tried to be nice to her—"

"I don't like Nancy," Trudy broke in, "and I wish you wouldn't talk about me as though I wasn't here."

"Trudy, that's not polite," her father said sternly. "She'll make friends when school starts."

School, and a thousand children! Trudy's stomach turned over, for school was one of the things she was trying to forget. She wished she were back in Vermont where she knew and liked everybody, and they liked her . . . where fences were built to keep cows in the pasture and not for spite, and where there were cats and kittens, all sizes, in Grampa's big barn.

She was much too big to tease and cry, but as she thought of the gray kitten, the warmth and softness of the tiny, furry body, the tears she would not shed backed up in her nose.

Her father, hearing a little sniff, passed her his handkerchief. "Don't feel bad, Frosting," he said. "Jean's right, you know. A trailer's no place for a cat."

"It's all right, Daddy." Moving away from Jean, Trudy snuggled against her father's arm. She wouldn't get the kitten—but he wanted her to have it. It was a very satisfying feeling to know that.

Sunday morning they attended church in the strangest-looking building Trudy had ever seen. Its towering walls were set at different angles, like piled up dominos. It appeared to have no windows at all, but inside it was flooded with light from above, and little flecks sparkled through thousands of small glass cubes which were set into the walls. One more thing to write home about!

She finished the long letter that afternoon while Jean was attending a concert with Mrs. Tripp, and Daddy was reading the Sunday papers. Trudy wrote on and on and on, but there were some things she did not mention. She sat at the desk for a long time thinking about them. Should she tell her father what Eric had said? What if Jean did not want her? What could he say?

As if her thoughts had conjured him up, she saw Eric sprawled on top of the Warrens' car.

Standing in the doorway, she called, "Come here. I want to ask you something."

He did not move, so she walked over, determined to grab an ankle and pull him down, if necessary. He saw the glint in her eye and slid to the ground.

"Was it true—what you said about her?" She bobbed her head toward the trailer. "Did she really say she didn't want me?"

He looked at the ground, trying to catch a piece of grass between his toes. "She said she didn't want you yet."

"Yet? What do you mean, yet?"

He shrugged. "I dunno."

"Who did she say it to? My father?"

"Sure." He started to walk away, but Trudy walked right along beside him, step by step. "What did he say?"

"Oh, you'll just love Frosting!" He said it in a high mocking voice.

Trudy went back determined to talk to her father, but just then Jean came back, thrilled with the concert and looking prettier than ever in a green suit and a huge straw hat.

She made a delicious rarebit for supper, which they ate by candlelight.

"What did you do all afternoon?" she asked Trudy.

"I finished my letter. And I talked to Eric."

"To Eric?" Jean looked annoyed. "Mrs. Tripp gave me a glimpse of his background this afternoon. He is definitely a maladjusted child, and it's no wonder, with his mother working and his father in Germany."

"What about the brother?" Trudy's father asked. "Didn't he run away or something?"

"Yes. The whole family is erratic. Mrs. Tripp says Barry is a bright boy, but his high school marks were so poor no college would accept him. He fell in love during his

senior year, and that didn't help. Then he wanted to enlist, but he's only seventeen and his mother refused to sign
the papers. She wanted him to go to prep school."

"Which would probably be a waste of money," Trudy's
father said.

"It seems so. Anyway, instead of going to school, he
went to New York, but he is not at the address he gave
them. That's the worst of it because after he left, Mrs.
Spear discovered her valuable necklace was missing.
They think Barry took it."

"I thought they were poor. How did she happen to
have a valuable necklace?" Trudy asked.

"It was an heirloom. Their grandfather Spear had
money. When he died, it came to them. And what do you
suppose Mrs. Spear did? She took Lorraine to Hollywood,
hoping she would become a child star. The father was
terribly angry. They say he asked to be transferred to Germany, and he has stayed there ever since."

"Did Mrs. Tripp say anything about Eric?" Trudy
asked.

"She thinks he knows where Barry is, and what became
of the necklace, too. They questioned him for hours, but
he sealed up that tight little mouth and refused to talk.
I don't want you to have anything to do with him, Trudy.
He can't be trusted."

Well, that was something to think about as they
watched television that evening. Her father and Jean sat
on the sofa; Trudy curled up in a big chair. I bet Jean
wishes I wasn't here, she thought, and stubbornly stayed
up until they made her go to bed.

It had been a long, long day... and yet she did not want it to end, for tomorrow was Monday, and Monday was school.

# 8: *School Begins*

"You look lovely, dear." Jean smiled approvingly that Monday morning at Trudy's flushed cheeks and satin-smooth hair, and the new blue gingham dress, so crisp and cool. "Have you got everything? School cards? Lunch money? Handkerchief?"

Trudy had everything, and Nancy Tripp was there to escort her to the right bus, and through the right door at school. That was a help, for the long low building had doors, doors, and more doors. They hurried down the tiled corridor to the principal's office.

"Wait here," Nancy said. "She'll come in a minute. I don't have lunch when you do, but I'll meet you out in the front at the close of school."

Trudy would never forget that first morning in the new school. Hundreds of children passed by while she stood there waiting. Finally, the principal came, looked at her cards, asked for her Florida address, how long she was staying, and her father's present employment. All the time she was talking, she was studying the pink card from the Vermont school. The marks were all A's but Trudy began to feel anxious.

Then the principal smiled and said, "Come with me, Gertrude." They walked down the corridor and through an open door. Trudy found herself facing a roomful of staring eyes.

"Miss Mullis, Gertrude Frost from Vermont." She lowered her voice but Trudy caught snatches, "country school," "good marks," "try her for a week and see."

Try her for a week! The words pounded through Trudy's head all that terrible day. The books, the lessons, the songs, the way these children talked—everything was strange. Even the room was different, with movable chairs and tables instead of proper desks screwed firmly to the floor.

The lunchroom was enormous. The noise confused her. The playground was even worse.

Trudy wandered off by herself to the farther side and when the bells rang, came in by the wrong door. Completely confused, she sat down in the right seat, but the wrong room. The teacher was not her teacher; the girl in front was not the right girl.

She was friendly, though, and tried to help, but by that time Trudy could not even remember her teacher's name. Finally she was returned to Miss Mullis, red-faced and late.

Even then her troubles were not over. The only time she was called on, she had no idea what the teacher was talking about.

"Gertrude, have you had the New Math?" Miss Mullis asked.

Trudy stood up, conscious that all the children were looking at her. A red flush stained her cheeks.

"I don't understand," she said in a very small voice.

"It's really the same math with new terms. Take the book home and look it over. You'll have to work, you know, if you're going to keep up with this class. Isn't that right, boys and girls?"

They exchanged smiles and winks at the compliment.

A feeling of panic swept over Trudy as she turned the pages. It was all about sets, subsets and intersections, whatever they were. The class turned to their books eagerly, but none of it made sense to Trudy.

At last the school day was over. She hurried out to find Nancy.

"How did you like it? Who's your teacher?"

Trudy answered the easy question. "Miss Mullis."

"Really?" Nancy was surprised. "Then you're in the accelerated group with the eggheads!"

Trudy was sure she wouldn't be there long and she didn't want to talk about it.

Jean was on the patio, smiling a welcome, wanting to know how the day went. Trudy told about getting lost; but that she was on trial for a week and could never make it, was something she could not talk about to Jean or to her father, when he came home.

He was not fooled, though. He knew it was an unhappy and worried child who ate her dinner quickly, dried the dishes, and went back to her room to study.

School had always been easy for Trudy. She had never asked for help with her lessons and she didn't intend to now. As she read the first pages again, trying to understand why some of the sets were pairs and others weren't,

her thoughts snapped back to the Vermont school, and
Jimmy Plaisted. He was dumb, the dumbest boy in the
whole room. She had never had any sympathy for him . . .
until now. Now she knew how he must have felt as he
struggled with common denominators. It was such a horrible feeling to have everybody else see through it, and
not be able to yourself. She read on and on, growing more
bewildered each time she turned a page.

The following days were somewhat better, but Trudy
was still confused by the rushing and pushing of strange
boys and girls, who breezed past her as though she were
not there. And the New Math was still a jumble of words
and symbols. Even when the teacher explained it, Trudy's
thoughts kept flying off in all directions for the simple
reason that she was unhappy.

Maybe she was homesick, if being homesick makes a
tight, aching feeling in the top of your throat so that you
can't talk. And yet, although she read her grandmother's
letters over and over until she knew them by heart, she
did not want to go back to Vermont. She wasn't a quit-
ter. She wanted to stay. But the feeling of anxiety, of
something being wrong somewhere, remained with her
and she could not shake it off.

Along with the worry about school, was the certainty
that Jean did not like her. Trudy kept remembering
things: the way Jean had looked when they bought the
swimsuit; the silent drive to the beach; the night when
she was sick and it was only the carpet Jean was concerned about. And now the kitten, the poor little kitten

would be drowned, probably, because Jean cared more for the Laphams' furniture than she did for anything else.

Even when she tries to be nice, Trudy thought, as she rode home on the bus that Wednesday afternoon, she's only nice on the outside. Inside she doesn't like me. And inside I don't really like her.

These were not thoughts to write home about, so again she wrote post cards to the family, telling them things they would like to hear. She wanted them to think she was happy, perfectly happy.

As she walked to the office to leave the cards on the counter with the outgoing mail, she saw Maida and Nancy playing croquet. Jimmy was tying his little dog, Tex, to a tree, and Eric was waiting for him beside the shuffleboard court. Trudy bought an ice-cream cone and sat down in the shade to watch the boys play.

Just then Lorraine came across the grass with Polly and Pam. They, too, stopped at the shuffleboard court.

"Polly, you stay here," Lorraine said. "Pam and I are going to play croquet."

"Aw, she'll be in our way," Eric complained, but Polly stayed and Trudy noticed that every time Polly wheeled her doll carriage across the court, he took her by the hand and led her back so she wouldn't get hurt. Even though he was not polite like Jimmy, he wasn't all bad. She finished her cone and went nearer.

"Want to play?" Jimmy asked.

"Yes, if you'll show me how. I've never played."

Eric muttered and scowled, but he stayed through one

game just so he could knock every one of Trudy's disks out of position. Then he took Polly back to Lorraine, and stayed to torment Maida, who couldn't hit a ball ten inches away.

Trudy concentrated on her own game and Jimmy said she made very good scores for a beginner.

That night Jean had roast chicken with fluffy whipped potatoes, squash, cranberry sauce, hot rolls and apple pie. Her husband praised her to the skies and kissed her twice.

"Trudy, we'll do the dishes," he said. "Jean's worked hard today." He led her to the divan as though she were a queen. Humph! Trudy thought, what's so special about cooking a chicken and making a pie? Jean had used every pot and pan in the kitchen and there was no place left to put anything down. But Trudy washed them all, getting angrier every minute. Then she went to her room to study. It was no use. The more she read, the more confused she became. She undressed, turned off the light, and lay down with her head at the foot of the bed so she could see her father stretched out in his big chair, reading the paper.

After a while he laid it aside and turned to Jean. "I wish she'd talk to us instead of keeping her troubles bottled up inside."

"It's the big school, Alan. When I changed from a little country school to the big one in Denver I can remember how scared and unhappy I was. But I got over it in a couple of weeks."

"Maybe it's the school, but I think she's homesick. She

hasn't acted natural since the day we went to the Raymonds."

"She was angry that day because she couldn't have the kitten, but girls of her age go from one enthusiasm to another. They think they'll simply die if they can't have a certain thing. Then that's forgotten and they want something else. Actually, Trudy is just beginning to discover herself as an individual."

Trudy almost fell over the end of the bed trying to hear her father's reply. But it was Jean who continued: "Apparently her grandmother always gave in to her. Just think of buying that expensive taffeta dress, for an eleven-year-old girl to wear in a trailer park. Child psychologists believe it is perfectly normal for children to want their own way. In Trudy's case, it would be strange if she didn't, because she's always had it. Alan, you'll have to admit that."

"No, I don't think so," he said slowly. "I don't think she's been spoiled. I think fundamentally she's a real sweet kid. It may be the big school. She has always been the big toad in a small puddle. Now she finds herself relatively unimportant, sort of lost in the crowd. But she has plenty of good old Vermont spunk. She'll come through all right. Just give her time."

"Darling, of course. She'll adjust. I'm not blaming her, and I'll do everything I can to make her happy."

"I know you will, dearest."

Dearest! Trudy buried her face in her arms. Jean was dearest; she was a toad. He only wanted Jean.

For a long while she lay there wide awak
miserable. Then the other things they'd said be
through. She smiled in the darkness for if it w
normal to want her own way, it opened up a
ant possibilities. She got into her bed the right
to think about them and soon fell asleep.

It seemed hours later that something aw
She heard a door open and close. Wriggling
end of the bed again, she balanced on her h
could look into the living room. A man was sta
holding a small carton.

"Alan, come here," Jean called. "It's Mr. Ra

"Hi, Alan. We're going away for a coup
so I'm taking the kittens down to the nigh
at Fishermen's Wharf. He'll take all he can
granaries and feed factories attract millions

The two men stood with their backs towar
she could see Jean's face, stern and pale, as M
went on, "Trudy wanted this gray one so ba
to take it down there and then find you'd ch
minds."

There was a flash of pink, as Trudy rush
father and threw her arms around the b
please don't let him go to the wharf! The
bigger than he is."

"The watchmen will take care of him in
until he's big enough to fight," Mr. Raymon
"It's really a good place. The cats get plenty
...only a house is better, of course..." His
off as he looked from Trudy to Jean.

hasn't acted natural since the day we went to the Raymonds."

"She was angry that day because she couldn't have the kitten, but girls of her age go from one enthusiasm to another. They think they'll simply die if they can't have a certain thing. Then that's forgotten and they want something else. Actually, Trudy is just beginning to discover herself as an individual."

Trudy almost fell over the end of the bed trying to hear her father's reply. But it was Jean who continued: "Apparently her grandmother always gave in to her. Just think of buying that expensive taffeta dress, for an eleven-year-old girl to wear in a trailer park. Child psychologists believe it is perfectly normal for children to want their own way. In Trudy's case, it would be strange if she didn't, because she's always had it. Alan, you'll have to admit that."

"No, I don't think so," he said slowly. "I don't think she's been spoiled. I think fundamentally she's a real sweet kid. It may be the big school. She has always been the big toad in a small puddle. Now she finds herself relatively unimportant, sort of lost in the crowd. But she has plenty of good old Vermont spunk. She'll come through all right. Just give her time."

"Darling, of course. She'll adjust. I'm not blaming her, and I'll do everything I can to make her happy."

"I know you will, dearest."

Dearest! Trudy buried her face in her arms. Jean was dearest; she was a toad. He only wanted Jean.

For a long while she lay there wide awake and very miserable. Then the other things they'd said began to filter through. She smiled in the darkness for if it was perfectly normal to want her own way, it opened up a lot of pleasant possibilities. She got into her bed the right way around to think about them and soon fell asleep.

It seemed hours later that something awakened her. She heard a door open and close. Wriggling down to the end of the bed again, she balanced on her hands so she could look into the living room. A man was standing there holding a small carton.

"Alan, come here," Jean called. "It's Mr. Raymond."

"Hi, Alan. We're going away for a couple of weeks so I'm taking the kittens down to the night watchman at Fishermen's Wharf. He'll take all he can get. Those granaries and feed factories attract millions of rats."

The two men stood with their backs toward Trudy, but she could see Jean's face, stern and pale, as Mr. Raymond went on, "Trudy wanted this gray one so badly I hated to take it down there and then find you'd changed your minds."

There was a flash of pink, as Trudy rushed past her father and threw her arms around the box. "Daddy, please don't let him go to the wharf! The rats will be bigger than he is."

"The watchmen will take care of him in their shack until he's big enough to fight," Mr. Raymond explained. "It's really a good place. The cats get plenty to eat. Only ...only a house is better, of course..." His voice trailed off as he looked from Trudy to Jean.

"Daddy," Trudy said softly, putting her arms around his neck the way Jean did, "please say yes. I want the kitten. I want it very much."

"I'm sorry, Frosting," he said, "but Jean was right. A trailer is no place for a cat."

For a long, long minute the soft whirr of the air conditioner was the only sound in the kitchen. A bright red spot burned on Jean's cheeks as she said quietly, "All right, Alan. You want her to have it. Let's keep it for a week and then decide."

"Daddy, that's just what the principal said about me. She'll keep me a week and then decide, and I can't do the New Math—it's about Unions and Equivalents and things I've never had."

He held her close. "Don't worry, honey. We'll help you. You'll get along all right."

"And the kitten, too?"

"We'll see. Now go to bed."

But still she stayed, because when Mr. Raymond let him out of the box the kitten ran into a floor cupboard near the refrigerator.

"Leave him alone. He'll come out," Mr. Raymond assured them. "When I get back, I'll take him off your hands if you don't want him. I came late hoping Trudy wouldn't know. You won't hold it against me?"

Jean laughed a very short laugh. "I'm sure you meant well," she said. He left soon after that and she turned to her husband. "Oh, Alan, how can we take trips to Miami and Cape Kennedy and Sarasota if we have a cat? We can't leave it here and we certainly can't take it with us."

"Nancy'll take care of it," Trudy called.

"Trudy, go to sleep," her father ordered.

"We can't let him outdoors without a leash. That's one of the rules of the park. I wish I'd said No and stuck to it." She got down on her knees and looked in the closet.

"Don't worry. Trudy'll take care of everything. If problems arise, we'll meet them one at a time."

"All right. Come and meet your first one." Jean stood up. "Your precious kitten's inside the refrigerator."

"What?" Trudy saw her father open the refrigerator door.

"Alan, don't try to be funny. He's in the back among the wires and fuses and machinery that make it go." Jean's voice rose higher and higher.

Trudy watched as her broad-shouldered father tried to squeeze into the small closet. When he stood up again, his face was very red. "You're right. The back's open. I'll unplug it and wait for him to come out. You go to bed. Both of you," he added sternly as he saw Trudy.

"Here's the carton the waffle iron came in. That should do for tonight," Jean said.

He put newspapers in the box, poured the cream off the top of the milk and set a saucer on the closet floor. Then he sat down at the dinette table to read Trudy's Math book.

Jean, in a wispy blue robe, came back to say good night.

"I've seen baby-sitters," she said, "but this is the first time I've ever seen a kitten-sitter."

Trudy smothered a giggle and jumped into bed. Jean

wasn't really angry. Daddy would explain the New Math. And the kitten would be good. She was sure of that.

In a few minutes she was sound asleep, dreaming of a school room where she was the teacher, and in every seat there was a gray kitten purring away.

# 9: Poor Purrky

WHEN TRUDY WOKE on Thursday morning, she found the kitten in his box on the patio, mewing for his mother.

"You poor baby," she said softly, "why didn't you drink your nice milk?"

"Trudy," Jean called, "it's late. Leave the kitten alone. Comb your hair and get dressed. The bus will be here before you finish your breakfast."

"All right." But she lingered one more minute because she knew how frightened a kitten must feel all alone in a strange house.

After school she rushed home to play with him. He went to sleep in her lap, so she picked up the Math book to study.

"Would you like me to help you?" Jean asked.

"No. Daddy said he'd help me."

"He had to go to Orlando. He'll be late tonight. Come on. We'll start right at the beginning and read it together." They did and soon it began to make sense.

"Thanks, Jean," Trudy said an hour later. "I see through it now. I can do it by myself."

"Good! If only you'd told us about it that first day, you'd have had nothing to worry about." Jean smiled, but

Trudy shrugged her shoulders and walked away. It wasn't quite that simple.

Friday, for the first time, she looked forward to the math period as eagerly as the other children did, and she enjoyed it.

That afternoon Nancy came over with a little collar for the kitten. "Isn't he cute! Have you named him?" she asked.

"I'm going to call him Purrky, P-U-R-R-K-Y."

"That's a perfect name, just like Frosting's perfect for you, because you're sweet and you look like frosting."

Giggling happily, they took the kitten out on the grass and lay down in the shade facing each other, arms and knees enclosing a little space where the kitten could play. He was so small he could slip his head out of the collar, but they watched him every minute.

"Don't *ever* let him go near the fence," Nancy warned. "If he went on Miss Kimberly's side you'd never get him back."

"Yes I would. I'd go after him."

"No, Frosting, you mustn't go over there. If she ever sells her land, my father wants to buy it. That's why the Triangle children must never trespass or annoy her. We want to keep as good feelings as possible."

While the kitten slept on Trudy's chest, Nancy chattered on about the families in the park, including the Spears.

Everybody knew about the missing necklace, she said, and she thought Eric had it, because he had a little box hidden away somewhere, and he wouldn't tell anybody what was in it.

"Do you think Barry stole it and gave it to him to keep?"

"No. Barry would never do a mean thing like that." Nancy's eyes grew dreamy as she talked about him. All the high school girls were crazy about him, she said, and Carol Davis, Rodney's sister, was really in love, but her mother said she was too young to get engaged. They had sent her to college in California, as far away as possible, so she'd meet other boys and forget Barry.

"Was he in love with her?"

"Yes." Nancy sighed. "He left for New York the day after she went away."

"Maybe he went to California."

"No. Her mother went with her, by plane. Carol and Barry promised not to see each other for a whole year. Do you think seventeen's too young to be in love?"

"I don't know." Trudy had never thought about it before. "Isn't it strange that Barry's so nice and Eric is such a horrid boy!"

"Well, Lorraine's always pestering him. She can't seem to let him alone. He does do awful things. The Verazzis can't stand him because he went into their studio and turned a lot of pictures upside down."

"I'll take you over there tomorrow," Nancy promised. "It's a separate trailer. Maida has wonderful parties there. She's having one next week. They invite children of other artists whom her father knows."

"Are you going?"

"Yes. Rodney, Lorraine, and Jimmy are, too. Maybe she'll invite you."

"I wish she would. I have a party dress. Want to see it?"

The kitten was soon back in his carton, and the dress on display.

"I haven't worn it yet." Nancy was properly impressed.

On Saturday she took Trudy to the studio and that was something else to write home about. It was no wonder Eric was tempted to turn the pictures upside down. They were gorgeous blobs of paint, like children's finger painting.

Mr. Verazzi was a real artist; he had long black hair and a beard. His wife wore tight green pants and her hair looked like a bleached haystack.

Trudy was terribly polite, but no one mentioned the party.

"I couldn't very well ask in front of you," Nancy explained, "but I will. And I'll ask the Coltons if you can go to the circus. It's in November at the college where Mr. Colton works. The students put it on. Last year he took ten of us and did we have fun!"

When Nancy went home, Trudy went with her, carrying the kitten to show to people as she strolled past their trailers. She stayed a long time at the Coltons' to let the little girls hold him and dangle strings for him to chase. She told Mrs. Colton that any time Lorraine couldn't come, she would be glad to look after them. She went home feeling happier than she had for days.

In fact, the whole week end and the days that followed were very happy ones for her and Purrky. On Wednesday, she took reading and language tests, but they were nothing to worry about. She knew she did well, finishing before the time was up.

She told Nancy about it on the bus.

"Yes, but wait until you get the arithmetic. Those problems! I hate problems!" They squeezed over to make room for Maida.

"I do, too," Trudy acknowledged.

Both girls went home with her to see Purrky, and they found he had a problem of his own. He was in a big carton with a screen and stool across the top, mewing sadly in protest.

"Go out and take him with you," Jean said. "He has been a perfect nuisance all day long."

"What did he do?"

"What didn't he do! He climbed right out of that carton and it took me forever to catch him and that wasn't fun in this heat. Then I let him in and see what he did?" She showed the girls the fragments of a Chinese bowl.

"Oh, my goodness gracious!"

"Trudy, I wish you wouldn't say that. It's utterly senseless."

"My grandmother says it all the time," Trudy retorted.

Jean bit her lip and walked away.

Trudy turned to the girls. "Let's go swimming. We can take turns holding Purrky."

"Okay. Wait for us to change."

"Whew!" Trudy said as she peeled off her sweaty clothes, "I never knew any place could be as hot as this in October."

When Jean did not reply, she felt a twinge of conscience. Gramma may have been easy in some ways, but she would never have tolerated a saucy answer.

Trudy stopped on her way out to say, "Jean, I'm sorry about the dish."

"We can never replace it. Oh, Trudy, I've had an awful day. I tried to make a strawberry chiffon pie and the beater jammed. I had to do it by hand and it hasn't hardened yet. And the kitten cried for hours without stopping, and Jimmy's mother said it cried all yesterday afternoon when I was out." She helped Trudy pull a rubber cap over her braids. "I'm sorry I snapped at you."

"I'm sorry I was saucy. Why don't you lie down and cool off?"

"I think I will. I'm afraid we're going to have a thunderstorm."

"That's good. It'll cool off then."

"Oh no, they're terrible here. I'm always frightened."

"I'm not. I like them."

The girls came then and Trudy picked up the kitten and headed for the pool. But even when she was diving and swimming, and especially when it was her turn to lie on the grass with Purrky, her thoughts kept going back to Vermont.

It would be cold there now. Grampa would have apple logs in the fireplace for Gramma to touch off when she sat down to watch television and do the mending. Her workbasket was always full of the family's socks, from the babies' to Grampa's. She was always busy.

Jean was so different! A new thought struck Trudy. Maybe *she* was lonely and restless sometimes. Maybe she'd like to be a secretary again .. if Trudy wasn't there.

"But it's not my fault," she mumbled, handing the kitten over to Maida.

"What isn't your fault?"

"You wouldn't understand." Trudy jumped into the pool and swam underwater to cool her head.

When she returned to the trailer, supper was on the table.

"Oh gosh, sandwiches again?" she asked, as she dropped her wet suit in the shower stall. "Isn't Daddy coming home?"

"He'll be late."

"Oh." One of the strange things about Jean was that she never prepared a real dinner unless her husband was there. She seemed to think a sandwich or cereal and fruit was enough for her and Trudy.

"What would your grandmother have on a hot night like this?" Jean's voice was pleasant, but Trudy knew her feelings were hurt.

"Cold chicken, hot biscuits, maybe applesauce or peaches, and molasses cookies."

Through the window she saw Jimmy knocking a golf ball around on the grass.

"Want to play?" he asked.

"Yes." She grabbed a sandwich, pushing the runny pink

pie aside, and ran out onto the patio. "Want to see my kitten?"

"Don't take Purrky outdoors again," Jean called. "See how dark it's getting."

"I won't." But Jimmy was already on the patio, with Eric right behind him. It wouldn't hurt to let them see Purrky, so she moved the screen and took him from the carton.

Then things happened fast. Tex, Jimmy's dog, dashed out from under the car. He jumped at Trudy. The kitten flew out of her arms, Tex ran after him, the boys after Tex, Trudy after the boys, dodging this way and that as Purrky disappeared among the petunias.

Jimmy caught Tex's leash and dragged him to their car, where he scratched at the windows, barking furiously.

Added to this noise and the boys' shouts was the rumble of thunder. Jean came hurrying toward them as a sharp flash streaked across the sky. "Trudy, why did you let him out? Your father telephoned. I'm going to meet his bus. Do you want to come with me?"

"No. I'm going to find Purrky."

Trudy squeezed through the hedge to look at the fence. There were plenty of places for a kitten to crawl through.

"He's gone into Miss Kimberly's garden," she moaned.

"He could be behind somebody's trailer," Jimmy said. "I'll ask everybody to look."

Trudy and Eric kept up the search. When Jimmy came back, Nancy was with him, but no kitten.

"I'm going to Miss Kimberly's," Trudy announced.

"No, you mustn't," Nancy said. "I've already called the radio station."

"What for?"

"When Polly was lost once they broadcast it. Miss Kimberly heard it and sent her gardener out to look, and he found Polly and brought her back."

Trudy hesitated. The sky had turned a horrid copper hue. The clouds hung so low they seemed to touch the treetops. A moment later there was a sharp flash, and torrents of rain came down. The ground that had been so hard and dry was suddenly ankle-deep in water. The children huddled under Jimmy's awning, watching as the park lights came on in the sudden darkness.

"The minute it stops I'm going over there. Nancy, won't you please go with me?"

"No. I certainly won't."

"Jimmy?"

"No. I promised Mr. Tripp I wouldn't."

"I'll go alone then. I'll go right to her door and ask permission to look for my kitten."

"I'll go with you," Eric said.

"You will? All right." It was better than going alone.

"May I wear your boots, Jimmy?"

Trudy looked at him, barefooted as usual. "What for?" she asked.

"I don't want to step on a snake."

"Are there snakes in there?"

"Water moccasins. They come out when it rains."

"Cut it out, Eric," Jimmy ordered. "You're just trying to scare her. You've never seen any snakes around here."

"I have, too."

"The rain's letting up," Trudy interrupted. Pulling off her sandals, she waded to her own trailer, where she put on Jean's boots and raincape, took her father's flashlight, the remaining McIntosh apples, and went outside again.

"I have a present for Miss Kimberly—apples from Vermont. They'll be a good excuse for bothering her," she explained.

"Trudy, if you go over there, you're no friend of mine. You'll frighten her on a night like this," Nancy declared.

"No I won't."

As she and Eric splashed down the driveway and out onto Kimberly Lane, lightning cracked right over their heads and every light in the park went out.

"Give me your flashlight," Eric said.

"Have you ever been there before?"

"Lots of times."

She followed him along a winding path bordered with bushes that drenched them as they passed. Again lightning made a frightful crack as it found its target in a tree nearby, and in the second of the flash Trudy saw a big square house with pillars supporting an upstairs balcony. Then thunder shook the ground under her feet, and the darkness was ten times blacker than before.

Eric found the steps and she stumbled up after him. They could see a faint light in one of the rooms. They called Miss Kimberly's name, and knocked loudly on the door.

"Maybe she's deaf," Eric said. "Let's go around the back."

He went ahead and she followed, still clutching the apples, tripping over unseen branches, sloshing through puddles, calling Purrky at every step, hoping if she made enough noise it would scare away those terrible snakes that might be slithering through the grass. Perhaps it did, for she didn't step on any.

They knocked on the back door and called again. Then Trudy took hold of the doorknob. It turned in her hand.

"Eric, it isn't locked."

"Open it."

"She wouldn't have a gun? And think we were robbers?"

"I dunno."

For a minute, standing there in the dripping darkness, Trudy wished she hadn't come.

"Are you going in?" Eric asked, "or are you scared?" Trudy opened the door and called, "Miss Kimberly, I'm looking for my kitten."

There was no answer. They stepped into the kitchen and stood there, dripping.

"Look," Eric whispered, flashing the light around. "There's a dish of milk."

It gave Trudy courage. "Please excuse us for coming in like this. Nancy Tripp told us not to bother you, but my kitten came through the fence to your side." As she talked she was tiptoeing to the small room where the light was.

The lightning struck again. Terrified, Trudy tripped over a rug and squeezed the rain-soaked apple bag so hard that it burst. Rosy McIntosh apples came bouncing

out. Some of them rolled across the room to the feet of a gray-haired woman who sat beside a table where a candle burned.

"Miss Kimberly, I'm Trudy Frost from the trailer park. If you found a little kitten, it's mine."

The woman stood up. "Don't shout," she said. "I'm not deaf. You're dripping all over my Chinese rug." She opened a SATURDAY EVENING POST and laid it on the floor. "Here. Stand on this." Then she opened a copy of LIFE for Eric.

"Where's Purrky? We saw the dish of milk—"

"That's my cat's milk. She's hiding upstairs because she doesn't like thunderstorms. I don't either. That's why I let you in. For company."

Flickering candlelight threw weird shadows over the woman's wrinkled face and straggly hair. Trudy picked up all the apples she could reach from her paper island and put them in what was left of the bag.

"These are a present for you. Is it all right if we look for Purrky in your yard?"

"No, it isn't. I don't want you over here, any of you. If I find the kitten I will let you know. You are the first trailer specimens I have seen so close. She inspected them from top to toe. Trudy glanced at Eric, who looked like a drowned rat with boots on. She wondered if she looked any better herself.

"No one has called on you because of the fence. They think you don't like them."

"I don't. This property has been in my family for nearly a hundred years. Then the State slashed a highway through my woods and a downright unscrupulous agent sold the triangle land to trailer trash."

"They aren't trash. They're nice people."

A scornful sniff was the old lady's reply.

Trudy reached over and poked Eric. "We'd better go. I apologize for bothering you." She poked him again.

"Me too," he muttered.

Miss Kimberly looked at him more closely. "Boy, what do you see?"

"Your minerals."

"Do you know what they are?"

"Agatized coral."

"Well, I am surprised." She lifted the candle to throw the light on a shelf where stones were displayed—in a variety of shades, shapes and sizes. "Do you know where they came from?"

"Tampa Bay."

"Remarkable. It always amazes me when a boy knows anything." Bit by bit, answering her questions, Eric told how the coral was changed—as trees in the petrified forest have been changed—to a substance like stone.

For once, Trudy was speechless. She watched Eric as he talked. His long wet hair was plastered to his scalp; his shirt and dungarees clung to him like a second skin, but his face lit up as he answered Miss Kimberly's questions.

"How do you know all this?" she asked.

"My brother. We used to live in New Jersey. There are lots of minerals there. He used to exchange stones with other guys."

Trudy hated to break in, but she was interested in her kitten, not minerals. "Eric, we ought to go," she reminded him.

"Eric, you are an intelligent boy, and it has been a pleasure to talk to you. I shall send for you to come again and bring your brother. I should like to see his specimens, and show him mine."

"He isn't here now, and he sold his minerals."

"Then I shall send for you. It is a long time since I have had the pleasure of meeting a young rock hound."

Eric grinned. "Sure. I'll come."

She opened the front door for them. "If I see your kitten I will let you know."

"Thank you," Trudy replied. Eric muttered something and took a flying leap down the steps. The rain had stopped.

"She liked you," Trudy said, running to keep up with him.

"Gooky old woman."

"Don't say that. She was nice."

He made the funny noise in his throat. "You don't have to tell everybody what she said."

"All right. I won't, but do you know what I think? You've got minerals in that box."

"What box?"

"Lorraine told Nancy—"

"They're gooks. Both of them. Two gooks."

"So are you." She put an end to his nonsense for just ahead, coming to meet them, was her father. "Daddy, we didn't find Purrky. Has he come home?"

"No. But whether you found him or not, you should not have gone to Miss Kimberly's when Nancy asked you not to."

"Miss Kimberly didn't care. She was nice. And were we polite! We apologized for bothering her, didn't we Eric?"

He nodded cautiously, not quite sure whether he could trust a gooky girl to keep her word, and ran off to his own trailer.

Again and again Trudy and her father searched the grounds. It was after eleven when he made her go to bed, after one last look for a poor little kitten, outdoors, alone in the wide, wet world.

# 10:  The Trial Period Ends

TRUDY WAS OUT AT FIVE the next morning calling Purrky, but he did not come. On the bus she told the children, and they said that they, too, would look for him.

When the time came for the remaining tests, it was a shock. Her mind had been so full of more important things that she had forgotten all about school.

Spelling came first, then arithmetic and the problems she had been dreading. "If a farmer sold apples at $3.50 a bushel wholesale—" She could see red apples rolling across Miss Kimberly's floor. Purrky. Where could he be? Was he lost and hungry? Or drowned in a big puddle? Jean would pretend to be sorry, but she wouldn't really care. She'd be glad. Trudy sighed and went back to the test. It was no use. She could not concentrate.

"Pass me your booklet," the teacher said.

"I haven't finished," Trudy protested.

"You knew it was a timed test. You should have been working, not looking out of the window."

Trudy went to the lunchroom with a heavy heart. Everything was wrong. Everything in the whole world. A big tear rolled down her cheek and plopped into the spaghetti. Sniffing hard, she lifted her chin and saw two girls rushing toward her.

98

"Trudy," they called, "the principal wants you. Somebody has found your kitten."

"Really?" She flew down the slippery corridor and skidded to a stop outside the office door.

"Your mother telephoned," the principal said. "Miss Kimberly is there with your kitten. She wanted you to know."

"Oh thank you! Thank you very much."

Trudy went right to her room and found herself telling Miss Mullis and the children who had come in early about being homesick and wanting the kitten, and her stepmother's thinking a trailer was no place for a cat, but she'd be willing to try it for a week, and all about Purrky's being lost, and found.

"We've both been on trial," she said, her cheeks very pink, "but now I'm sure Purrky can stay. Jean would never send him away after last night. And I hope I'll pass my tests so I can stay here with you."

Trudy saw a freckle-faced boy point to the door. The principal was standing there, smiling. "You needn't worry, Gertrude. You passed the tests. This is your room. We hope you will stay with us and finish out the year."

Miss Mullis and the children clapped, and the freckle-faced boy pounded on his desk.

Trudy's voice squeaked as she told them how happy she felt. Then she went to her seat, the seat that was really hers. The week on trial was over. The weeks of belonging had begun.

On the bus she told Nancy and Maida the good news, and at the Triangle invited all the children into the store for double-dip ice-cream cones.

I've got a lot of things to celebrate today!" she said happily. "Come home with me and see Purrky. You too, Eric," she added as he hung back.

He tagged along at the end with Polly and the doll carriage.

Jean met them on the patio. "What's this?" she asked. "A parade? A party?"

"It's a celebration. This is my lucky day. I've passed my tests, and the kids are glad. They clapped and clapped. Where's Purrky?"

She stopped to wrap an extra napkin around Polly's cone which was melting all over her hot little hand. "Careful, hold it up straight. We're going to see the kitty in a minute. Where is he? He hasn't. . . Oh, Jean, he hasn't run away again?" Trudy stepped past her into the living room, the stream of children following. "Where is he? Where's Purrky?"

"Now don't get excited," Jean said quietly. "Miss Kimberly has taken him home with her."

"Why? What for?"

The silence seemed to last forever. Trudy watched Jean as her eyes flicked uneasily from one face to the next, from Jimmy and Maida, carefully licking their cones to keep the excess under control; to Nancy, listening intently so she could repeat every word; to Eric; to Pam; to Polly, just as she laid her cone on a magazine and began to move her dolls to the sofa.

Polly smiled at Trudy. "Now I'll put the kitty in my carriage and take him for a ride."

"You can't, Polly. You can't ever take him for a ride

again." Trudy's voice was loud and harsh. "Jean has given him away. My kitten." She turned, eyes blazing. "You had no right to do it. Mr. Raymond gave him to me. My father wanted me to have him."

"Trudy, please listen. Your father's going to Miami—"

"I don't care if he is and I won't listen." She stamped her foot so hard the little teacups rattled on the shelf. "You never wanted the kitten. I suppose you'll get rid of me next. You never wanted me."

Jean's face was white. "Trudy, please don't say that. You were to keep the kitten until you made friends. Now you have friends at school and all these nice children." She looked at Polly's melting cone and still managed to smile. "Wouldn't you rather have your kitten in Miss Kimberly's lovely home than have Mr. Raymond take it away?"

"No! He was mine. To keep. You had no right—"

"Children," Jean interrupted, "you'd better go now. I want to talk to Trudy, to try to make her understand."

"I'll go with them," Trudy said defiantly, "and I wish I never had to come back as long as you're here." She swept Polly's dolls off the sofa and dumped them into the carriage. "Come on. She doesn't want us."

"Trudy, wait. Please let me talk to you," Jean pleaded, but Trudy rushed out of the trailer and the other children followed.

"Now we're going to Miss Kimberly's," she announced.

"Oh, Trudy, don't start that again," Nancy begged.

"Why not?"

"You know why not. You ought to be ashamed of being

so rude to your stepmother. Come on, Pam, Polly." She linked arms with Maida and the two little girls obediently went with them.

"Jimmy? Will you go with me?"

"I've got to take Tex for a walk."

"Eric?"

He wriggled uncomfortably and wiped his mouth with his fist. "I'm going with Jimmy."

All the fight went out of Trudy as she watched her friends go their different ways. She was exhausted, lonely with a terrible loneliness, and ashamed, too. She shouldn't have said that to Jean. It wasn't right. Worse than that, it wasn't true.

Her longing for her grandmother was so acute that at the moment it crowded out everything else. She was hardly aware that her feet were taking her down Kimberly Lane; she was surprised to hear someone call, "Where you going, Miss?" and to see Miss Kimberly's gardener coming across the grass.

"Is Miss Kimberly home?"

"No, she's gone out."

"Do you know where my kitten is?"

"He's in the shed. He's all right."

"Can I see him? Please?"

"You kin look in through the screen door, but I wouldn't open it 'cause she won't like that. You go look at your kitty. Then you go home. She don't want trailer kids over here."

Trudy went down a little garden path to the shed. Inside she could see a few chairs, a table and a couch.

"Purrky," she called, "come, kitty, kitty."

She saw him then, the poor little lonesome thing. There was no reason why she shouldn't hold him for a little while. She reached up and lifted the hook, bracing her knee against the door, then knelt to open it. Suddenly an enormous gray cat burst through, banging the door against her forehead with a stunning blow.

She picked Purrky up and sat down on the coarse, stubbly grass. A lump was swelling from her eyebrow to her hair. By tomorrow she'd have a black eye. One more trouble! She held Purrky against her chest, her chin on his soft fur. But Purrky had ideas of his own that day. He wriggled and tried to get away, mewing so persistently that she put him back in the shed and hooked the door.

"Even my kitten doesn't like me," she said aloud. There was no one to hear, no one to care. Why? Why was she here alone? She had always liked people and they had liked her. She had always been the lucky one. Now nobody liked her.

She wandered around rubbing her head and looking for the big cat.

Bright orange butterflies flitted among the hibiscus blossoms. Birds sang in the trees. It was such a lovely place. Why couldn't she be happy?

She walked along the fence, still calling the cat. She did not find it, but she did find a loose board in the fence that could be pushed out, leaving a hole big enough to crawl through. Crouching, she stepped out of the Kimberly garden, squeezed past the punk trees and found the way back to the trailer.

It was too early for dinner, but she was hungry. She decided to get her handbag and buy some cookies. She opened the door quietly, hoping Jean would not hear, but no such luck.

"Trudy, wait," she called. "I want to talk to you." Then she saw the lump on her forehead. "Good heavens, what happened?"

"I bumped my head," Trudy said coldly.

"Let me put something on it."

"You needn't bother. I came for my handbag. I'm going to the store."

"No you're not. Come here, into the bathroom."

Trudy stood still while Jean wrung out a face cloth in cold water and placed it on the swelling.

"Hold it there while I make a compress with chipped ice." That done, she took Trudy by the hand. "Come. Sit here on the sofa. I must talk to you. I'm sorry I sent the kitten away without telling you first. I shouldn't have done it."

"Why talk about it? You didn't want the kitten. You don't want me."

"I have never said I didn't want you." There was a long silence before she added, "But it was the truth. I didn't at first."

Trudy felt an icy shiver, colder than the compress, tingle down her spine. Without speaking, almost without breathing, she watched Jean, who was turning her wedding ring around and around on her slender finger.

"I was nervous, dismayed is a better word, at the idea of being a stepmother."

It was almost as though she had forgotten that Trudy was listening. She looked away from her toward the sprinkler that was whirling a rainbow of mist into the rays of the setting sun. "I love your father very much. I want him to be happy. When this Florida assignment came through, his first thought was of you. 'Now Trudy can come and live with us,' he said. And because I loved him so much I said, 'Yes, I want her, too.'"

She turned toward Trudy and spoke more slowly. "I had hoped for a little time before you came to try out my cooking, for one thing, because I had never done any. I knew I would be nervous with you watching. I did not want to make mistakes. But I was ready to love you. I wanted very much to make you happy."

"Then why did you give away my kitten?"

"That's what I want to explain. While Miss Kimberly was here, your father telephoned. He was afraid you'd never find Purrky alive, and he planned this trip to Miami to take your mind off it. We'll pick you up at school tomorrow and drive down the west coast and over the Tamiami Trail. Won't that be fun? We couldn't do it if Miss Kimberly hadn't offered to take the kitten."

"You mean for the week end? Why didn't you say so?"

"No. She's going to keep him. We cannot have a kitten here."

"Why not?"

"If we let him in, he'll ruin the furniture. If we leave him on the patio, he will cry and annoy everyone. We're all too close together in a trailer park. Oh, Trudy, why can't you understand?"

Trudy stuck out a stubborn chin and said nothing.

"Miss Kimberly likes cats. She has a big gray Persian that is very valuable, but it's old and deaf, so she never lets it out."

"It's valuable? It's... it's big?"

"Yes, and very friendly, so your kitten will have a good home and good cat company, too."

Trudy turned the compress over, but it no longer eased her aching head. She looked at Jean, wishing she could snuggle into her arms and say she was sorry, that she loved Daddy, too, enough to do anything...anything to make him happy. And what...oh what should she do about the Persian cat? But the words wouldn't come.

"Miss Kimberly does not want you running over there," Jean added, "but sometimes she will invite you to come and see Purrky."

"Did she say anything about Eric?"

"She said he was interested in her minerals. I told her about his background, and that he couldn't be trusted—"

"Why did you have to do that? She liked Eric, and he can be trusted."

"No; I don't think he can. Isn't it true that it was something he said that made you think I did not want you?"

"Who told you that?"

"Nancy said—"

"I hate Nancy. She's a...she's a gook." Trudy jumped to her feet and the teacups danced again. "She's always telling everything she knows."

"I've noticed it myself." Jean smiled, sure that the worst was over. "Oh, Trudy, I'm thrilled about this week end!

I've only been to Miami once and I've always wanted to go again."

"And that's why you got rid of Purrky so fast." Trudy was not quite sure why she said it. It was as though some second, hateful self was determined to keep her unhappy. "Maida's having a party Saturday. I'd rather go there."

"You would?"

"Yes I would." Trudy scowled, blinking back bitter tears.

"When your father calls I'll tell him. He'll not be home tonight," Jean said wearily. "I'm going to lie down. You can make another compress if you want to, and find something for your supper." She went into her bedroom and closed the door.

Trudy found chicken and applesauce in the refrigerator, and homemade molasses cookies in the cake box. It was a good supper, but her appetite had gone.

Too tired to make another compress or even wash her face, she lay down on her bed. Jean found her there, still asleep, in the morning.

# 11: A Secret Shared

Nancy stared at Trudy as she boarded the bus the next morning. "What happened to you?" she asked.

"I was hit by a door."

At school she gave the same explanation adding, in reply to the children's other questions, that her stepmother had given Purrky away. Maybe they thought Jean had hit her. All right. Let them think so.

And yet, that was not fair. "I love your father very much. I was ready to love you." The words kept ringing through Trudy's head. She had been ready to love Jean, too, but had she ever let her know it? Had she ever really tried to be a "good" girl, the way Gramma meant it?

I will try, she resolved, because if I make her happy it will make Daddy happy. She bit the eraser on her pencil, stared at the sky and thought about it a while. She could understand why Jean had not wanted her "yet." Eric's word made sense now. But she should not have sent Purrky away. She should not have told Miss Kimberly that Eric could not be trusted.

And yet, Eric was to blame for much of Trudy's unhappiness. Her thoughts circled from Jean to him, to Maida's party, and back to Jean.

Schoolwork could not hold her attention that day. The

first one on the bus when the dismissal bell rang, she hurried home to start being nice to Jean. However, Jean was out. She had left a note saying she was playing bridge with the Massachusetts ladies, and there were date-nut cookies in the tin box.

Trudy grabbed a handful, changed to slacks, and went through the fence to Miss Kimberly's shed. The door was open and the shed was empty.

She decided to find Miss Kimberly and tell her the whole story. At the corner of the house, she met the gardener. Yes, he said, the big cat had come back, but Miss Kimberly was plenty mad. "You go home and don't bother her no more. How'd you get in here, anyhow? You climb over that fence?"

"No. Where's my kitten?"

"In the house, but Miss Kimb'ly don't want you trailer kids around. Now you go home." She went, because he stood and watched her until she did.

Well, the cat and the kitten were safe. Now to make sure of her invitation to Maida's party.

She found the girls playing croquet. "When we go shopping, I'm going to buy a dance record for Maida's Hi Fi," she confided to Nancy while Maida took slow and careful aim at the farther stake.

"Why?"

"For her birthday."

"Her birthday's in May."

"Oh. I thought it was a birthday party. She knows I'm coming?"

"Does she? Did she invite you?" Nancy took her turn

and walked to the next wicket. Trudy tagged along after her.

"You said she would. You said you'd ask her to."

"I changed my mind. Why don't you ask her yourself?"

"It wouldn't be polite."

"I'm surprised that that bothers you."

Flinching from the insult Trudy walked away, but her determination to go to the party was unshaken. After upsetting plans for the Miami trip, she had to go. Maida was her friend. She must have intended to invite her.

Trudy sat down under the palm trees to think of a polite way to bring up the subject. She was still thinking when she heard her father call her name, and there he was, with Jean.

"Daddy! I didn't know you were home." She ran to him and hugged him hard. "Oh, I've missed you so."

"I know, Frosting. I'm sorry about the kitten, but Jean was right. We couldn't keep him here. You understand, don't you?"

"Yes, Daddy." She waited, expecting a scolding. Instead, he praised her for her success at school, said he was glad she was invited to Maida's party and, since she was going, he and Jean had accepted the Warrens' invitation to play golf on Saturday.

"You're not going to Miami?"

"Jean suggested we postpone it until next week end."

"For my birthday! I'd love that!" She threw her arms around Jean whispering, "Thank you for not telling him. I'm sorry. I won't be rude again."

"I knew you didn't really mean it, dear."

As her father talked about the trip, ideas began popping in Trudy's head. One was nothing less than an inspiration.

"May I ask Maida to go with us? I'd like to do something nice for her."

"I think that would be lovely," Jean agreed.

"Oh boy! I'm going right now." The girls had left the croquet grounds, so she ran across the grass to Maida's trailer.

Mrs. Verazzi opened the door and she could see through Trudy as though she was a pane of glass. Maida had ballet on Saturday mornings, she said, and could not possibly go to Miami. And the party was planned for sixteen and it was too late to change. She was sorry, but they were very busy. Trudy found herself outside without exactly knowing how she got there.

She decided not to tell her father and Jean. She knew they would not leave her alone for a whole day with nothing to do. And she wanted them to play golf at the Country Club, and have fun.

She felt a little sad and very noble on Saturday morning when they drove away.

It was a long day. She tried to read. She started a letter but there was not much that was pleasant to write about so she started a picture puzzle. After lunch she watched the children arriving at the studio. She saw Jimmy go in, and Nancy in a new red dress, and Lorraine, wearing a tight green sheath and very high heeled shoes

After a while she stole out behind the bushes to listen to the dance music. She loved to dance. She loved parties.

It was a terrible experience to be on the outside, looking in.

She had absolutely nothing to do. Too restless to keep still another minute, she decided to go and see Purrky. No one would ever know.

She crept through the fence and waited to make sure that the gardener was not around. A twig snapped and she froze. Something . . . or somebody was moving on the other side of the shrubbery. Standing on tiptoe, she caught sight of a khaki shirt. It was a boy. It was Eric! He took a few steps, listened, looked around, went on again and disappeared.

Trudy waited, not daring to move. There he was, near an old dead tree hung with festoons of Spanish moss. He put his hand into a hole, took it out again, and walked away.

"Eric!" she called.

He jumped as though he had been shot. "What do you want?" he growled as she untangled herself from the bushes.

"I came to see Purrky."

"I thought you went to the gooky party."

"I wasn't invited."

He scowled at her without speaking.

"What did you put in the tree?"

"Nothing."

"That's a lie." She took a step nearer.

He moved to block her way. "Keep away from there."

"You can't stop me." For a minute she thought he was going to try. Perhaps he remembered how strong her hands were, but Trudy decided, as she thought about it afterwards, that he really wanted to share his secret with someone.

"Let me see. I promise not to tell." She edged nearer, put her hand into the deep hole where an old limb had been torn away, and brought out a package.

"Give it to me," he ordered.

She passed it to him. He untied a string and removed two plastic bags that had once covered bunches of carrots.

"I didn't want it to get wet," he mumbled, showing her a small leather box, about three inches square, two inches deep, hinged and locked.

"Where's the key?"

"I don't know."

He turned it over, breathed on it, and rubbed off a spot of mildew on his pants.

"Is it the necklace your mother lost?"

"No." He pinched his lips together, glowering at her.

"Where did you get it?"

"Barry."

"Where did he get it?"

"He always had it."

"What's inside?"

"A piece of quartz." Trudy smiled encouragement as though a piece of quartz was something special. Eric went on, "It's full of amethyst crystals. Barry's going to give it to me if I keep the box safe while he's gone."

"Real amethysts?"

"They will be when they're cut and polished." There were a lot of minerals where they lived in New Jersey,

he said, so Barry collected them and traded with other people. Eric rattled off names: franklinite, calcite, rhodonite and a dozen others, while Trudy stared, mouth and eyes wide open in admiration.

"Goodness gracious! Are they all in that one little box?"

"No." Eric was disgusted at her ignorance. "Minerals take up a lot of room. When we moved to the trailer, Ma made Barry get rid of most of his stuff. But then he began collecting coral—"

"Yes, you told Miss Kimberly about that. What I want to know is what's in there besides the amethyst thing?"

"I don't know. But it's valuable. Barry said so."

"Why didn't he take it with him?"

"He.. he thought it would be safer here."

"But not in a tree, Eric."

"Lorraine knows about it and she's always hunting—"

"Let me take it. My father will keep it for you in his office safe."

"Nothing doing."

"Where's Barry now?"

He waited a long time to answer. "New York."

"You don't think he went to California?"

"No. He didn't go to California."

"Let me take it for a minute?" She examined the box. Then she shook it. "I bet your mother's necklace is in here."

"I told you. It isn't. Barry wouldn't steal."

"He needed money to go to New York."

"He had money. He worked on a fishing boat all summer. He earned almost a hundred dollars a week."

"Maybe that's what's inside. Hundred dollar bills folded up tight. Let's open it and see."

"Open it? No." He looked as horrified as though she had suggested cracking the safe in the Tampa bank.

"If Lorraine finds it she'll open it," Trudy argued, "and if the necklace should be there—"

"It isn't. I keep telling you."

"Do you know where it is?"

He shook his head. "I wish I did."

He looked so troubled that Trudy felt sorry for him. "Eric, you needn't worry about me. I'll never tell." Solemnly she crossed her heart and drew a finger across her throat.

"You'd better not if you know what's good for you. Now I've got to find another place to hide it."

"You needn't. I wouldn't steal any more than Barry would." Apparently he believed her, for he put it back in the tree.

She followed him through the fence and into the trailer park. Only then did she remember that she had not even looked in the shed to see if Purrky was there.

The party was over. She saw Lorraine and Rodney sauntering across the Triangle, hand in hand, as she sat down on the patio to finish her letter to Vermont.

A few minutes later, Lorraine joined her.

"Maida's mother was mean not to invite you to the party," she declared. "She was probably afraid you'd get all the attention. Maida's such a dope. She freezes every time a boy looks at her."

For five minutes she talked about the party, then

changed the subject. "I'd like to see this trailer. I've never been inside."

"Come on in." Lorraine looked and raved. Everything was gorgeous, utterly gorgeous. She lingered in the doorway, looking at Jean's dressing table where her make-up box lay open.

"Trudy, let me make you up. If I darkened your brows and lashes you'd be a living doll."

Trudy giggled. "Could I wash it off?"

"Of course. It'll only take a few minutes. Sit down. Open your eyes wide. Now close them. Don't blink. Hold still."

"Jean only uses a little tiny bit."

"You need more than that. When I get through you'll be as stunning as she is. What does she use on her hair?"

"Nothing. It's really natural."

"She's lucky. My mother used to be pretty. Now she doesn't care how she looks. She's too fat. That's one thing I'll never be." Lorraine worked as she talked. "I'm concentrating on your eyes. Your complexion is perfect. Just a touch of lipstick, and look!"

Trudy looked and was amazed. "My stars! Is it really me? I do look sixteen! Do my hair up like yours."

Using Jean's comb and hair spray, Lorraine teased Trudy's hair into a high swirl. "How do you like it?"

"It's gorgeous! I'm going to put on my party dress. This is fun!"

"Maybe I'll find something, too." Lorraine slid the closet door open and took a blue lace dress from Jean's rack.

"You're already dressed up," Trudy protested.

"This old thing? I've had it forever." It was off, and Jean's dress was on. Trudy felt it was wrong of Lorraine to do it, but Jean would never know. In her own room, she slipped the pink taffeta over her head carefully, then surveyed herself in the long mirror.

"I knew it," Lorraine gushed ecstatically. "You're a doll! By the time you are sixteen, every boy who sees you will go mad, utterly mad."

"You look nice, too."

Lorraine changed the subject as though she had turned the dial on the television set. "Did Eric show you the box? Don't look so surprised. It's no secret. Did he show you what's inside?"

Trudy was caught. She should have known that Lorraine was up to something with all that soft soap, as they called it in Vermont.

"You needn't lie to me," Lorraine went on, putting both hands on Trudy's shoulders. "It's my mother's necklace, isn't it?" Her long fingernails dug into the soft hollows in Trudy's neck.

"Ouch! You're hurting me." She grabbed Lorraine's wrists and flung her off.

Her voice softened then. "My mother's terribly worried. She thinks Barry stole it."

"Barry wouldn't steal."

"Oh? So Eric talked. What else did he say?" Lorraine walked into the living room, sat down in the big chair and put her feet on the hassock. "I'm staying until you tell me. Let them come home. I don't care."

Trudy wanted to scream, to fight, to tear Lorraine into

little pieces, but how could she without ruining Jean's dress? She sat on the sofa, very still, and tried to think.

Lorraine yawned. "I can wait as long as you can."

Trudy watched the clock, fidgeting and perspiring. She would never tell Eric's secret. But she'd better wash off the mascara before her father and Jean came home. When she stood up, Lorraine came after her, but Trudy darted into the bathroom and locked the door.

She started to wash, then stopped, afraid she would soil the dress. She tried to pull it over her head, but the zipper caught in her hair. She was still struggling when she heard a car stop, and her father's voice.

With a tremendous yank, she pulled the dress free and ran out of the back door crying, "Daddy, Daddy, Lorraine's in there and she won't go home."

"Holy mackerel! What happened to you?"

He stared at her as she stood there in her slip, her tousled hair falling over one ear, her mouth a crimson gash, her eyes smudged and sultry.

"What have you been doing?" Jean demanded, "playing Cleopatra with that awful make-up?" Then, as Lorraine came gliding out, she moaned, "Alan, look! She's wearing my wedding dress. Oh no!"

"I haven't hurt it," Lorraine said apologetically. "Trudy wanted to dress up, kid stuff, and I did it to please her. She was so disappointed because she wasn't invited to Maida's party."

"I was not."

"What are you talking about?" her father interrupted.

"Mr. Frost, she's been over in Miss Kimberly's woods all afternoon with Eric—"

"What?" Trudy had never seen her father so angry.

"She knows where my mother's necklace is. I wish you'd make her tell me—"

"I don't know. Oh, Daddy, make her go home." Turning toward him, Trudy burst into a flood of tears.

"Hey, don't come any nearer," he warned as black rivulets coursed down her cheeks. "Go inside and wash that stuff off your face."

Using innumerable cleansing tissues, Trudy finally got cleaned up. She combed her hair and came out for the scolding.

Her father was waiting for her. "Begin at the beginning. Were you invited to that party, or weren't you?"

"Daddy, I thought she was going to invite me—"

"But she didn't, and you knew it before we left. You deliberately planned it so you could go to Miss Kimberly's—"

"No. I didn't tell you because I wanted you to play golf—"

"Trudy, I find that hard to believe."

"It's the truth."

"But you went to Miss Kimberly's."

"Yes, but I didn't bother her. She didn't even know, because I went through a hole in the fence."

"Oh, Trudy, how could you?" Jean broke in. "And to go with Eric Spear—"

"I didn't go with Eric—"

"That's enough," her father said sternly. "You're not

to snap at Jean like that, or talk to her the way you did last week. No, she didn't tell me. She didn't need to when all the children in the park heard your outburst."

"I'm sorry. I didn't mean it."

"And I suppose you didn't mean it when you painted your face and let that girl wear Jean's wedding dress?" He paced back and forth, hands behind his back, while Trudy stood against the door, her lower lip stuck out, scowling as hard as she could.

"Look at me," he said at last. His face was troubled. His eyes held hers until she looked away. She could meet anger with anger, but when he turned gentle and kind and sad, she began to melt inside.

"I didn't think you'd act this way," he said slowly. "You were such a happy child when you lived with your grandmother. You weren't rude and disobedient. What has happened to you?"

She didn't know herself, so she pinched her lips together and said nothing.

"Aren't you happy here?"

It was a hard question to answer. She shrugged her shoulders and stared at the second button on his shirt.

"You had better go to your room and stay until supper is ready. And remember, you are not to be rude to Jean ever again, and you are not to trespass on Miss Kimberly's property."

"And keep away from the Spears," Jean added.

"I'll keep away from Lorraine. I hate her. But Eric needs a friend," she said stubbornly. "You...you just don't understand."

"Talk to us, dear. We'll try to understand," Jean said gently.

They stood together, watching her, waiting for her to speak. It was so quiet in the room, she couldn't stand it another minute.

"I want to go home," she burst out.

"Do you really mean it?" her father asked. "Because if you do—"

"Yes, I mean it." A flood of emotions swept over her —love, jealousy, anger, loneliness.

She turned quickly and her head struck the shelf that held Mrs. Lapham's precious bone china teacups. Before she could catch it, one fell to the floor and broke.

"I don't care," she cried defiantly, and then, because she really did care so very much, and because everything she did was wrong anyway, she kicked it.

"Trudy, go to your room," her father ordered.

"I'm going," she sobbed, as she went.

# 12: *Two Letters to*

# *Vermont*

SUNDAY WAS A LONG SOLEMN DAY. Trudy was quiet and exceedingly polite but inside she was wound up like a coiled spring. She went to church as usual with her father and Jean, and to dinner in Lakeland, and then to a concert at the college there.

When they returned home, they found the couple from the Ohio trailer waiting on the patio. Trudy had met them before and found them very boring, so she went to her room to finish the weekly letter to her grandmother.

The page she had already written had the good news about her tests at school and the children clapping. What else was there to write about except troubles? Purky's getting lost and found and being given away, and Lorraine and the eye shadow and mascara. Gramma would be horrified at that, but Trudy's pen was soon racing over page after page. Pressure built up as she wrote, and out came all the troubles she had been keeping to herself for weeks.

The letter ended with a cry from the bottom of her heart. "I've been rude and disobedient," she wrote, "but Gramma, they don't understand children and I'm homesick for you. Can I come home? Please." She underlined it four times, assured them of her love, addressed and stamped the envelope and took it to the office right away.

No one was there, but Mr. Tripp was just outside.

"Where's Nancy?" Trudy asked.

"She has gone with her mother to collect for the Red Cross or something."

An idea that had been floating in Trudy's head for some time suddenly crystallized. "May I use your telephone?" she asked. "We have company and I do not want to disturb them."

"All right, if it isn't a toll call."

"No, it isn't a toll call." She looked up the number, dialled, and heard Miss Kimberly's voice.

"This is Trudy Frost," she told her. "How's Purrky?"

"In good health apparently. Is that what you called for?"

"No. Wait, Miss Kimberly, please. I want to tell you about Eric." Talking as fast as she could, Trudy explained that Jean was wrong. Eric could be trusted and she hoped Miss Kimberly would ask him over to talk about his minerals because he knew about all the different kinds, and about amethyst crystals, too.

"Most people don't like him," she said in conclusion, "and that's why he needs friends. My stepmother doesn't understand children or she would never have said what she did. He can be trusted. He is a very honest boy."

"And you are his champion. I appreciate your good intentions, Trudy, but please don't bother me with any more telephone calls." The phone clicked in her ear. Trudy replaced the receiver and took the long way home.

The visitors had left. Jean was pouring batter for waffles and bacon was crisping under the broiler. After supper they all worked on the picture puzzle Trudy had started until Jean remembered that her husband had promised to look at the Ohio lady's television set.

"Want to go with us, Trudy?" her father asked.

"No. I'm tired. I'm going to bed."

She went to bed but she wasn't tired. Throughout the evening she had had an uneasy, restless, all-gone feeling. With the writing of the letter her anger and resentment toward her father and Jean had completely melted away. She wished she hadn't written all those awful things. The more she thought about it the more she realized that she didn't want to go back to Vermont. She knew it now for sure, sure, sure.

There was another thing, too. What would her grandparents think when they received it? She tossed and turned and buried her face in her arms as she pictured Gramma watching for the mailman, hurrying down the driveway, and calling Grampa to come in so she could read Trudy's letter to him.

"Goodness gracious," she'd say, "I thought she was getting along all right." Grampa wouldn't say anything, but he'd take his pipe and go back to the barn to smoke and think it over. They would not tell the family until they had to, she knew, because Vermonters don't tell everything they know, especially unpleasant things. She had to get that letter back or it would make a lot of people unhappy.

Impetuous, as always, she sat up and pushed her feet into her sandals, threw on a robe and made a beeline through the dewy grass to the office.

It was still open and the outgoing mail was on the counter. Mrs. Tripp sat at her desk, making out bills.

"What do you want?" she asked, not pleasantly at all. There was no doubt that Nancy had given her an earful about Trudy's misdeeds.

"Would you please give me back the letter I wrote to my grandmother? I want to change something."

"You can take it. It's right there on the counter."

"Thank you very much, Mrs. Tripp." As Trudy slid off the top post cards and letters to find hers, she drew in her breath quickly for there was a second letter for Mr. and Mrs. Joseph C. Frost, Pottersville, Vermont, and the handwriting was Jean's.

She left quickly, cheeks burning, two letters clutched in an icy fist. She put them in the bottom drawer, under her clean clothes, and went back to bed.

There was little sleep for her that night. It took hours to persuade herself that what she had done was absolutely necessary. Her father wrote home occasionally; Jean never did. There was no doubt in Trudy's mind that the letter concerned her rudeness, and that they were sending her back. It would be much harder for Gramma and Grampa to hear about it from Jean than from Trudy.

She could tear up her own letter and throw it away. But Jean's...what should she do with Jean's? Destroy it, too? Steam it open and read it? No. She could never

do that. Tell Jean and beg her not to send the letter? Maybe if she made up her mind to do that, the awful pain in her stomach would go away. Yes, that was the best thing, the only thing to do. Having made the hard decision, she fell asleep.

She woke early and could hardly wait for the others to get up. When they did, she found Jean had decided to go to St. Petersburg and it was one of those congested mornings when everybody was hurrying and getting in everybody else's way. There was no time to talk or to listen to long explanations. Trudy took her own letter to school; Jean's stayed in the drawer.

Nancy sat with Trudy on the bus that morning. "I want to talk to you," she whispered confidentially.

Trudy's heart jumped into her throat. Mrs. Tripp had seen her take Jean's letter...she knew it...she knew it...

But Nancy was talking about something else. "You shouldn't have said what you did to Miss Kimberly," she began.

"Miss Kimberly? What do you mean?"

"I heard you tell her about Eric, and Jean's not understanding children—"

"How could you? You weren't in the office—"

"No, but I was in Miss Kimberly's house, with my mother. The telephone is right on the desk and you talked so loud—"

Trudy had had all she could stand. "I wish you'd mind your own business once in a while," she snapped.

"Don't say that. I'm trying to help you. Tell Jean about it, if you haven't already, because if you don't my mother's going to. She thinks you need to be disciplined. It won't be half as bad if you tell her yourself." Nancy seemed genuinely concerned.

"All right. I'll tell her."

"And I want to apologize for what I said about your going to Maida's party. We're sorry you weren't invited. We did ask her mother, but she said, 'No.' "

"It doesn't matter."

"It's too bad Maida can't go to Miami with you. She wants to, terribly. If you want me to, I can go."

"No, I'm not even sure I'm going myself." Anything could happen between now and Friday, and something bad probably would.

Trudy was sick in school that day, so sick she had to go to the nurse's room and lie down. Even then she had such a thundering headache that it hurt to move or open her eyes. At last she slept, and woke up feeling better.

As soon as her father and Jean came home, she gave them the letter Jean had written and, starting with the telephone call, told the whole story from beginning to end.

Her father explained the seriousness of tampering with the United States mail. Even though the counter was not a post office, and though people who left their post cards and letters there did so at their own risk, still a person who willfully took a piece of mail was committing a crime and could be severely punished.

"I know it. I'll never do it again."

"Where's the letter you wrote to your grandmother?"

"I tore it up."

"What did you write?" He took her by the hand and led her over to the sofa. "Try to remember and tell us everything. Perhaps it will help us to understand what's troubling you. We don't want you to be troubled, Frosting, you know that."

"I wrote about the kitten, and Jean, and Lorraine, and Eric." She paused to run her tongue over her lips and cough to relieve the tightness in her throat. "I said I was homesick and I wanted to go home, but I don't, Daddy, I don't. That's why I didn't send it."

"First you want to go, and then you don't. Aren't you a pretty mixed-up girl?"

"Not any more." His arm tightened around her shoulder and she snuggled closer.

Alan Frost smiled at his wife. "Well, Jean," he said, "shall we send this letter or not?"

"Well, Alan," she replied, almost as though they had a little private joke between them, "I think perhaps we could wait a while."

From then on Trudy was so sweet and obedient at home, so ready to help, so attentive at school, and so kind to everybody that she began to wonder why wings didn't sprout on her shoulder blades. And as if to prove that goodness is rewarded, at the very last minute the Coltons asked her to go with them to the famous circus at the college. She was overwhelmed with joy. She found the Triangle children packed in the station wagon, and

Nancy and Maida welcomed her as if she had always been their dearest friend.

When they drove past the store Trudy saw Eric there, watching them go.

"Why didn't they invite him?" she whispered to Nancy.

"They did. His mother wouldn't let him go because he had a fight with Lorraine. That's why they asked you."

Trudy pointed to the seat in front where Lorraine was cuddling close to Rodney. "But she let her go."

Nancy nodded. "It's never Lorraine's fault, not in that family."

It was too bad for Eric, but Trudy did not let it spoil her evening.

The circus was held in an enormous gymnasium. Students in sparkling costumes performed on the trapeze, swinging high under the vaulted roof. They did balancing acts, tight-rope walking, and trampoline bouncing which Trudy had never seen before.

A dozen clowns who kept falling off everything were the best of all. Or was the parade the best, with people inside the funny animals? Trudy laughed until she cried.

It was after midnight when they got home, but she had to stay up to tell her father and Jean about it. They were very glad she had had a good time, but they had disappointing news for her. The Miami trip was postponed again. In the morning her father was leaving for the West Coast.

"It means I won't be here for your birthday," he said. "I'm awfully sorry, but Jean will take you somewhere Saturday, perhaps to the Tampa Parrot Park."

"That's all right with me, Daddy."

"And we'll go to some nice place to eat," Jean promised, "and you can wear your pretty pink dress."

"I'd love that!" Trudy gave them each a strangling hug and ran off to bed.

# 13: A Birthday Comes
## and Goes

TRUDY DETERMINED to keep on being an angel while her father was gone—obedient, polite, and as nice to Jean as she could possibly be.

Crossing the Triangle the following afternoon, she passed Eric, all alone, pitching horseshoes. "Hi," she said to be polite, and walked right along, to be obedient.

To her surprise, Eric came over to talk. "We had an air-mail letter today," he said.

"From Barry?"

"From my father. Barry's with him."

"In Germany? How did he get there?"

Eric almost burst with pride. "On the UNITED STATES, the best and biggest ship there is. He earned his way waiting on table. He wanted my father to sign papers so he could enlist."

"Did he?"

"Nope. He made him go to school. But they're coming home in June to stay."

"I bet you're glad. Then you can give him the...the you-know-what. Is it still in the tree?"

Eric nodded. "I couldn't move it. That gooky dope's always watching me."

"Aren't you ever curious about what's inside?"

He lifted a horseshoe with the toe of his sneaker and balanced it on edge. "Sometimes."

A strange thought hit Trudy. In spite of his crazy actions, she liked Eric. He was an intelligent boy, discussing minerals with Miss Kimberly; a trustworthy boy, guarding his brother's box; a lonely boy, missing the circus, playing alone so often.

"Saturday's my birthday and Jean's taking me to the Parrot Park. Would you like to go with us?" she asked in a burst of friendliness.

He looked up, startled, then shrugged his shoulders. "Have you ever been there?"

"Nope."

"But you'd like to go."

He threw a horseshoe at the stake and missed by a yard. "I guess so."

"Okay. You're invited." Trudy smiled on him like a fairy godmother, her spirits soaring because she had brought happiness to this poor boy. Only, unfortunately, this poor boy was Eric Spear, and she'd have a tough job of explaining to do. She chewed her thumb thoughtfully all the way back to the trailer.

"Jean, do you believe in sharing happiness with other people?" she asked, as a good introduction.

"Yes, of course I do," Jean replied.

"Even if it's someone you don't like? Even if it's Eric?" Without giving her time to reply, Trudy explained what she had done and why, making out a very good case for the poor boy who had so little happiness in his life. "He has never been anywhere, and you'll like him when you know him better."

It was clear that Jean had doubts about that but, like Trudy, she was trying hard to keep things running smoothly. Since the invitation had already been given, she consented to take Eric along.

Birthday happiness was in the air. Cards were arriving from friends in Vermont. Trudy's class sent her their picture. A square box came "For Our Florida Frosting from the Family." Trudy ripped off the pretty wrappings and shrieked, "It's a camera! Wowee! I'm going to take pictures of you and the kids and the palm trees and everything!"

There was another box with a canary-yellow sweater knitted by Gramma, and a tiny pony with white blaze and feet, exactly like Pepper.

"From Grampa," Trudy said, balancing it on her hand. "Oh, Jean, they're a super-duperly wonderful family. Sometimes I miss them so, it hurts right here." She thumped her chest. "But I don't want to go back. I'd be ashamed to have them know . . . I couldn't get along in Florida."

Then Jean brought out another gift and Trudy opened the biggest box of all. Inside were a matching wool plaid skirt, jacket and shorts.

"Thank you," Trudy said quietly. "They'll be nice and warm."

"What's the matter?" Jean asked, disappointed at the lack of enthusiasm. "Don't you like them?"

"Yes, they're very pretty. But they're for Vermont, aren't

they? Oh, Jean, did you send that letter? Did you tell them I said you didn't want me . . . and . . . and everything?"

"Your father wrote that letter, Trudy. I added a postscript and wrote the address. I'm not sure whether he has sent it or not. But these clothes are for Florida. We'll have cool, damp days before the winter's over."

"Do you think he'll let me stay that long?"

"I think he will. He loves you very dearly. You know that. Remember, it was you and not he who suggested your going back. You said you wanted to go."

"But I don't."

"Not under any circumstances?"

Trudy was not quite sure what Jean meant, but she repeated the words, "Not under any circumstances."

That twelfth birthday was one to be remembered. It was what southerners call a pretty day, bright and pleasantly cool. Trudy wore her new shorts and sweater. Eric arrived half an hour early in a new shirt and chino pants, with a sleek and fragrant haircut, clean even to his ears and fingernails, and he was as good company as anyone could ask for.

Jean sat on a bench in the shade, leaving them free to run around and see everything. Trudy took pictures of the gardens, of the penguins on their make-believe iceberg, and of the pink flamingos with what looked like make-believe legs.

There were gorgeous mackaws, peacocks and lorikeets, toucans and pelicans—some in large cages, many flying free all over the park. There was a show of performing birds. Jean watched it with them once, the children saw it three times.

It was one grand and perfect day.

They went back to the trailer to rest and shower and change their clothes, but the evening was no fun at all. For one thing, a chill, thick fog settled in, making it hard for Jean to drive, so they went to the nearest restaurant instead of the nicest one. The real trouble was Eric. He was a changed boy. He looked nice, wearing his best jacket, white shirt and tie. But he would not talk. He wiggled and squirmed and stretched his neck out of his collar, sidewise, like a turtle, sighing so loudly that the waitress came over to see if he was ill.

He ordered a hamburger and glared at Trudy when she told him that was not proper at a birthday dinner. She was radiant in her lovely pink dress, her hair shining like pale gold, but he couldn't have cared less. He ate as fast as possible, wanting only to get out and go home again.

Jean and Trudy were talking about him the next morning at breakfast, wondering whether he had been embarrassed by the big dining room or whether his collar was choking him. They heard a knock at the door. It was Nancy, bursting with news. Eric was ill. Lorraine was telling everybody it was because he took a bath, but she was worried. Nancy could tell because when she telephoned for the doctor she could hardly talk.

He came that day and again the next day, and took Eric to the hospital and put him in an oxygen tent because he had pneumonia.

Little by little the truth came out. Just as he left for

Trudy's birthday dinner, Lorraine told him that she had found his little black box. Late that night he had stolen out of their trailer. She followed, lost him in the fog, came home, locked the door and went to bed. She had not intended to keep him out all night, but she had fallen asleep and he had not wakened her. The ladies in the Massachusetts trailer found him asleep in their car when they went to early Mass on Sunday morning.

No wonder the poor child had pneumonia, they said. The trailer park people could talk of nothing else.

Trudy was terribly upset. She was worried about Eric. She was worried about his box. Lorraine could not have found it, or she would not have tried to follow him. But she must know now that it was on Miss Kimberly's side of the fence. And she would keep searching until she found it.

The compulsion to go over there and get it herself so her father could keep it safe, was so strong that it haunted Trudy in the daytime and kept her awake at night. When a thing is right or wrong, a decision is not so hard to make. But here she was, bound by a promise not to go to Miss Kimberly's, and bound by her promise to Eric not to tell his secret. And while she did nothing Lorraine might find the box and open it, and keep whatever was hidden inside. Hour by hour Trudy moved in an absent-minded dream while her thoughts stayed in Miss Kimberly's woods, in a certain old, dead tree.

A few days later Mrs. Colton asked her to baby-sit with Polly and Pam since Lorraine was going to the hospital with her mother. Trudy was glad to do it.

When she got there, she found Polly in tears.

"She has lost a dime. If you can't find it, give her another one and put her to bed," Mrs. Colton said, searching for her gloves and car keys and hurrying out the door.

"Let's make it a game," Trudy said. "Dime, dime, where is Polly's dime? I'll look in this chair. You look in that one." They looked in chairs, pockets, corners. No dime, but no more tears. "Maybe it's in the doll carriage. Let's play house-cleaning and take everything out."

That took a long time because, in addition to dolls and stuffed animals, they found books, shells, broken cookies, melted caramels, and clothes, Polly's and the dolls'. She was happy again; Pam, too, as they played with long lost toys.

But Trudy had a tidy mind. "Why don't we finish the job?" she asked. "Get me some newspapers and I'll dump out the rest of the stuff and brush the carriage clean."

Out came the last blanket and pillow, the last broken shells, the last crumbs. Caught on one side was something that sparkled, something on a chain.

"What's this?" Trudy asked, pulling it out.

"It's my dolly's." Polly put it around her big doll's neck. "But it won't stay on. See?" She showed Trudy the broken clasp.

"Where did you get it?" She examined the delicate flowers, the exquisite workmanship.

"I don't know."

"Do you know, Pam?"

"I never saw it before."

"Did Lorraine ever wear it around her neck?" It seemed

improbable, but the stones looked like diamonds and rubies.

"I guess so." Polly picked up an old mechanical monkey and made it dance.

When the clean-up job was completed and the children were in bed, Trudy looked at the necklace again. It must be Mrs. Spear's. Lorraine must have worn it and lost it, and then accused her brothers of stealing. Trudy's indignation reached the boiling point. She could hardly wait to tell Lorraine what she thought of her, but their trailer was still dark.

She had to talk to someone so she called Jean.

"What is it? What's wrong?" she asked, arriving breathless at the door.

"See what I found in the doll carriage. Could it be the necklace Mrs. Spear lost?"

"It certainly could." Jean held it under the light; the jewels sparkled like fire and icicles.

"You just wait till Lorraine comes home," Trudy declared.

"Shouldn't you talk to Mrs. Colton first?"

"Yes, but I'm going to tell Lorraine—"

"Trudy, wait a minute. I don't like Lorraine any better than you do, but think what she must have been through these past weeks, knowing she had lost it and suspecting Eric had found it and put it in that box everybody's talking about. Sometimes I wonder if there is any box."

"There is. I wish I could tell you more but I promised Eric I wouldn't tell anybody."

"Then don't, but please don't get involved in any more of the Spears' troubles. Will you promise me that?"

"I promise." She looked straight into Jean's eyes and smiled.

When Mrs. Colton came home she was deeply concerned because she liked Lorraine, and if the necklace was her mother's it would mean more trouble for that unfortunate family. She agreed, however, that they should go to the Spears immediately, as the lights were on again. Their trailer was clean, but shabby. The springs in the sofa sagged; the linoleum was badly worn. Mrs. Spear had changed to a shapeless housecoat and sloppy slippers. She cried when they asked her how Eric was getting along.

"He was a little better tonight, but he's an awfully sick boy," she said, mopping her eyes. "The fever goes down, then it goes right up again. Last night he didn't even know me. My baby. My poor baby."

"We're sorry—very, very sorry," Jean said gently.

"Me too," Trudy added. "I like Eric a lot."

Lorraine, stacking dirty dishes in the sink, had nothing to say.

There was an awkward silence. Then Mrs. Colton asked, "Olive, is this your necklace? Trudy found it in the doll carriage."

"You found it... where?"

Lorraine turned sharply, beating a fist against her lips, her eyes wide with fright.

"In Polly's doll carriage. We were looking for a dime

and—" She didn't finish because Mrs. Spear collapsed on the sofa, sobbing hysterically.

"You took it, Lorraine? You lost it? Why didn't you tell me?" she moaned. "Oh, what I've suffered for my children! Barry gone. Eric at death's door. My daughter, my only daughter, a thief!" Tears streamed down her face and she trembled all over.

"We'd better go," Mrs. Colton whispered. "She'll cry a while and then she'll get over it. She's a very emotional woman."

"Poor Lorraine," Trudy said as she closed the door behind them. "I never thought I'd feel sorry for her, but I do."

"And for her mother, too," Jean added.

"Yes," Mrs. Colton agreed. "Olive Spear never understood her boys, but she adored Lorraine."

"People are very complicated, aren't they?" Trudy observed thoughtfully.

"I'm afraid so." Mrs. Colton sighed and went into her trailer.

Trudy slipped her arm through Jean's as they walked across the grass. Compared to Lorraine's, her troubles were insignificant. In fact, as far as they concerned Jean, she realized they were no longer troubles at all. That made a happy conclusion to an exciting evening.

# 14: The New Triangle

BECAUSE THINGS WERE TURNING OUT RIGHT Trudy decided, the very next day, to settle the one remaining problem. She would go through the fence for the last time, get the box, keep it until Eric came home, and make him give it to her father.

She was careful, watching for the gardener or Lorraine, who might still be snooping even though the necklace was found. In a fever of excitement she reached the tree. The box was there! She wanted to shout for joy as she raced back across the stubbly grass. In a few minutes she would be home to hide it and keep it safe for Eric.

But first she must say good-bye to Purrky. She called him and he came to the shed door.

"Good-bye, little pussy cat," she said, kneeling to tickle him under the chin as he rubbed against the wire. "It may be a long time before I see you again, but don't forget me."

She stood up, brushed the dirt from her knees and started toward the fence. Lorraine was standing there, watching.

"Give me my brother's box," she demanded, her eyes blazing.

Panic seized Trudy and she ran, not toward home, but away from Lorraine, away from the fence and Miss Kimberly's house. It would be hard to defend herself while holding the box and Lorraine was ready to fight, to hurt, if she could, with those long sharp fingernails.

Trudy tore across a sandy field of sparse, dry grass. Beyond she could see an orange grove. No place to hide. On the boundaries, palmettos, scrub pine. Far ahead, on her right, a brush pile, a thicket of vines and bushes, a few trees. She must reach it, dodge around and head toward home or Lorraine would drive her into the palmettos.

Not daring to look behind, she ran until she thought her lungs would burst. Gasping, she reached the brush and crouched low for a dizzy, painful second, waiting for Lorraine to close in on her.

But Lorraine was walking through the grove a few rows away. Why? Hadn't she seen her? Was she playing cat-and-mouse? Trudy wished she knew. She was in a horrible place with rotting wood all around and, not twenty feet away, palmetto scrub where even workmen would not venture without high boots to protect them from rattlesnakes.

She remembered Jody's father getting bitten by a snake in THE YEARLING. That snake had been on a grapevine. Trudy looked at the vines above her head, at the Spanish moss dripping from the oaks and the untidy

bark hanging in strips from the nearer punk trees—all good hiding places for snakes and hairy black spiders. She saw a lizard flat against a branch not ten inches from her face, and her stomach turned over.

If she didn't stop thinking of bugs and snakes, she would scream. She made herself watch a butterfly with yellow and black stripes across its wings, and a black wasp with a fat red tail. She made herself breathe more slowly, more slowly, more deeply. Then something moved in the dead leaves at her feet and she darted out like an Olympic racer, through the grove and across the grass to Miss Kimberly's yard, where she fell at the gardener's feet with a stabbing pain in her side.

"What's the matter? Somebody chasing you?" he asked. Then, alarmed when she could not answer, he called Miss Kimberly. They put wet cloths on her wrists and head and gave her water as soon as she was able to drink.

"Was that boy chasing you?" the gardener asked. "I told him to get out of here a hundred times."

"No, it was his sister." Later, when she could talk more easily, she told them where Eric was, and why. They helped her to her feet and, still holding her precious box, she thanked them and went home.

But now that she had it, where should she hide it? In her handbag? Nobody carries a handbag all the time. But people seldom locked their trailers unless they went away. And Lorraine was bold enough to walk right in.

During the days that followed Trudy moved that box from bag to bureau drawer, from shoes to skirt pocket, to every different, safer place that she could think of. At night she slept with it under her pillow. For Lorraine was prowling. Twice Trudy saw her under their windows. No wonder Eric was nervous living in the same trailer with her. No wonder he chose a tree for a hiding place.

And all the time Trudy's curiosity about what the box contained burned brighter and brighter. Was it just minerals? She shook it. She poked hairpins and paper clips into the tiny keyhole, wondering. Nothing worked. She hardly expected it to. She slid the flat blade of her scissors under the lock and pulled gently, then not so gently. The lock stayed locked, but suddenly the old leather gave way, the metal tore out, and the box was open.

"Gee-iminy!" she gasped. "Now I've gone and done it!"

Wrapped in tissue was a piece of rock shaped like a cupped hand. The inside surface was covered with pale lavender points. So that was the amethyst crystal. Trudy hardly glanced at it, for fitted in beside it was something far more interesting: a small white box. She turned it over in her hand. She opened it. It was lined with purple velvet and it held a diamond ring.

"Whee-ew," she whistled softly. Barry must have bought it for his girl friend and her parents would not let her take it. Trudy slipped it onto the fourth finger of her left hand to see it sparkle. The amethyst crystal meant nothing, but this beautiful ring she must guard with her life.

That weekend Trudy felt as though she were two different girls. On the surface everything was fine. She had received her first report card—all A's and the teacher's comment: alert and cooperative. All the trailer park people were her friends, except Lorraine. Eric was improving. Best of all, she and Jean were very happy together. So she should have been as carefree as a pet canary. Instead, she felt as though she were sitting on a barrel of dynamite that could blow her up, and the ring, too, at any minute.

On Tuesday her father telephoned to say that he was on his way home.

Jean picked Trudy up at school and they went to Tampa where Jean had an appointment at a beauty salon, after which they would go to the airport. Trudy spent the free hour choosing a picture puzzle for Eric, and gazing at store windows.

One was a jewelry store. There was a diamond ring, marked seven hundred fifty dollars. On the impulse of the moment, Trudy went inside where a pleasant-faced saleswoman stood behind the counter.

"Can you tell me how much this diamond ring is worth?" Trudy asked her, opening her bag.

The clerk called a man with a shiny bald head and showed it to him.

"It isn't mine," Trudy explained. "It belongs to a friend."

"Oh?" The man popped a magnifying glass into one eye and looked at the diamond, popped it out again and looked at Trudy. "It's a good diamond. Where did you get it?"

"I can't tell you. But I didn't steal it, if that's what you're thinking. Thank you. I just wanted to be sure." She held out her hand.

"Just a minute." He lifted his eyebrows at the saleswoman and she disappeared. "I think you'd better tell me where you found this."

"I didn't find it. I knew where it was."

"What's your name?"

"I'm not going to tell you." She looked him straight in the eye. He could not keep her ring. She knew that. But she wished with all her heart she'd never gone into that store.

"Just a minute." He examined the stone again, stalling for time.

"I've got to meet my mother." It was surprising how easily the word slipped out. "Give me my ring if this is an honest store, or I'll tell the police."

"There's a policeman right here. Come on."

Trudy followed him into a back room where dozens of watches hung on the wall. Tiny wheels, springs and screws lay among tools on a bench with bright lights hanging over it. The saleswoman was there and a policeman who looked about ten feet tall. He asked Trudy what was going on.

"He won't give me my ring."

"Yes he will, but young girls don't usually go around pricing diamonds. You wouldn't tell him your name. That made him suspicious. Now, suppose you tell us who you are."

She crossed fingers on both hands and said quickly, "Susan Elizabeth Blake."

He wrote it down. "Where do you live, Susan?"

"Miami."

"Father's name?"

"Robert. We've got to meet his plane. May I go now?"

"Who's we? You and your mother? What's her name?"

"Jean." It was like a cry for help. Trudy wanted her. This was too much trouble to handle alone. "She's having her hair done at the Bella Verda salon—" She stopped, bit her thumb. "Her name is Frost. She's my stepmother. Will you call her? Please."

"Stepmother. And her name is Frost."

Trudy realized she had blundered, but if only Jean would come nothing else mattered. However, no Mrs. Frost, no Mrs. Blake, had had an appointment at the Bella Verda.

"She took me there once. Maybe she went somewhere else today."

"Maybe she did." Before Trudy could stop him, the policeman had opened her handbag and was reading the identification card in the billfold: Gertrude Frost, Tall Pines Farm, Pottersville, Vermont: "Where'd you get this?" he asked.

"It's mine."

"For the first time I think you are telling the truth. Now listen, you can help us. There was a robbery last week at one of our big jewelry stores. Tell us where you got this ring and it may help us catch the thief."

"It won't help."

"How do you know?"

She closed her lips tight.

"Are you going to talk here, or shall I have to take you to the police station?"

"No. Please don't. Take me to the parking lot. Jean must be there and she'll be worried."

"Okay." They walked because it was just around the corner. The car was there; Jean was not. But the attendant said that a lady had been looking for a girl. Suddenly Trudy screamed and dashed across the lot. "Jean," she cried, "Oh, Jean, don't let them put me in jail!"

"Trudy, what's wrong? Where have you been?" Jean gasped.

"I showed him the ring that was in Eric's box and they arrested me." She clung to Jean as though she would never let go.

"Sorry, ma'am," the policeman said, "but she wouldn't talk, and a kid with a nice diamond ring—well, we want to know what's going on."

"Trudy, you can't keep Eric's secret any longer. Tell him what you know, and hurry. Daddy's plane is in already."

"Eric had to take care of it for his brother and he hid it in a tree. I promised not to tell." She bit her lips hard, ashamed of the dreadful thing she'd done.

"And you took it?" the policeman asked.

"Yes, because Eric's in the hospital and I want my father to put it in his safe. Oh, could...could you keep it a secret, too?"

"She is telling the truth, officer." Jean looked at him with her big brown eyes. "May we go now?"

"All right. I won't make any report. Only next time, tell the truth. Don't make up any fancy names."

Soon they were headed for the airport and caught in the late afternoon traffic. Trudy had plenty of time to tell Jean everything, and what a relief that was.

When at last they arrived, Jean looked for a parking space and Trudy ran to find her father.

He was pacing up and down by the telephone booths, hot, tired, and increasingly worried as time passed and Jean did not come.

"Hi, Daddy!" Trudy rushed into his arms, all out of breath.

"Hi, Frosting. Where's Jean?"

"Parking the car."

"What happened? Why are you so late?"

"Daddy, it was the policeman's fault."

"Policeman? What happened? Did Jean have an accident?"

"No, it was me. I almost got arrested. I went into a jewelry store with Eric's ring—"

"Eric's ring? Are you still mixed up with those Spears? Jean wrote that you took the boy to the Parrot Park—"

"Yes, we're trying to help him. We like him very much."

"Who's we?"

"Jean and I. Oh, Daddy, we get along fine now. At first she was nice to me and I was nice to her to make you happy, but now we like each other—just because we do. Oh, we've got so much to tell you!"

"Suppose you start with the policeman."

He looked so stern that Trudy's exuberance collapsed like a pricked balloon. For a whole week she had not thought once about being sent back to Vermont, but now she must face it again. "I get along all right until you come home," she mumbled, "then I get into trouble again."

"That's nonsense."

"It isn't nonsense. Here comes Jean. Ask her."

Jean tried, but she could not hide the fact that Trudy had gone to Miss Kimberly's again, taken Eric's box and opened it.

"Good heavens, Trudy, that was a terrible thing to do. The minute we get home you're going to take that box right over to the Spears."

"I can't do that. Eric's still in the hospital."

"You can give it to his mother."

"Daddy, you don't understand—"

"Stop arguing. Please. I've been working since five o'clock this morning and I'm tired."

They were all quiet, too quiet, during the drive home. Then he said, "All right now. Take the ring and the box and everything that belongs to them back to the Spears."

"Can Jean go with me?"

"Why do you want her to go?"

"Because Lorraine might be there and Eric doesn't want her to have it. That's why I took it. Can't you understand?"

"Jean's going to cook supper. Come on. I'll go with you."

He set off at a fast pace and Trudy lagged behind, still trying to think of some way out. There was none. He rapped on the door and Mrs. Spear opened it and asked them in. Lorraine was not there, which was one thing to be thankful for.

"Mrs. Spear," Trudy began at once, to get it over with, "I broke my promise to Eric. I took his box out of the tree to keep it safe for him. And I opened it." Her eyes brimmed with tears but she blinked them back. "The amethyst crystal is in here and Barry's diamond ring." She put the leather box in Mrs. Spear's hand.

"So that's where Barry's money went!" Mrs. Spear held the ring under the light to see the white flash of the diamond. "It's a nice one, isn't it! Don't feel bad, Trudy. When Eric's fever was very high he kept raving about the box, the box. He had to go and find the box. Then Lorraine told him you had it. He said, 'Her father'll keep it for me,' and we told him yes—and do you know, his fever went down and he went to sleep. That's when he started getting better."

"You will keep it in your safe at the office, won't you Daddy?"

"Why yes, I'll be glad to."

Eric's mother passed it to him. "It'll take a load off my mind."

"When is he coming home?" Trudy asked.

"The day after tomorrow. He wanted me to tell you about the book Miss Kimberly sent him. It's got nice bright pictures of all kinds of minerals. I've never seen Eric so happy. He said Trudy must have told her he was sick."

"Yes, I did. I have a picture puzzle for him at home. I forgot to bring it."

"Tomorrow will do for that," her father said. "Come on

home. I'm as hungry as a bear. I'll put the ring in my safe and give Eric a receipt. I'm glad to do it, Mrs. Spear. Good night."

Outside, he caught Trudy by one braid and pulled her toward him and walked her home, with his arm around her waist.

"All's well that ends well," he said to Jean as she opened the door. "Who do you suppose is the present guardian of the diamond ring?"

"You are. I'm so glad!" She and Trudy watched him put the box into an envelope, seal it and write his own name and Eric's on the outside.

"Now write the receipt," Trudy urged.

"This is to certify that I am holding, for safekeeping, one diamond ring, property of Eric Spear." He signed his name and the date.

"Now Eric won't have a thing to worry about." But Trudy still had a worry, and this seemed a good time to settle that, too. "Daddy, you didn't send that letter to Gramma, did you?"

"Yes, I did. Why?"

Trudy's face fell. Just when everything was turning out right, something bad always had to happen. "I didn't want her to know I'd been rude to Jean. Are you. . .are you sending me back?"

"Well—" He hesitated and for a second Trudy thought she saw a twinkle in his eye as he looked at Jean, but his face was very solemn as he turned to his daughter. "To tell the truth, I thought you were homesick. I thought it would do you good to go back to Vermont. That is what the letter was about."

Trudy sighed one of her long, sad sighs, as pictures flashed through her mind: Eric's face, Miss Kimberly's, her class at school, Miss Mullis, the game court and swimming pool, the Triangle Park children, Florida sunshine, birds and flowers, the trips, the restaurants, the cozy trailer, her father, Jean.

"When do I have to go?" she asked.

"Next week."

"Next week?" She bit her lip so hard that it hurt.

"I have made the reservation."

"Alan, stop teasing her," Jean ordered. "Trudy, honey, we're all going."

"What?" Her voice went from low C to high C in that one short word.

"Home for Thanksgiving! I wrote to your grandmother as soon as I knew there was a possibility of my being able to go. We waited until we were absolutely sure before telling you, so that you wouldn't count on it and then be disappointed." Alan Frost put one arm around his wife, the other around his daughter. "With all those A's we decided you could take a few days off from school."

"And I can come back here when you do?" Trudy asked.

"You're our Florida Frosting," Jean assured her.

"Oh Jean! Oh Daddy!" Trudy put her free arm around Jean, making a firm triangle. She was almost bursting with love for them both, with thankfulness and joy, and a dozen promises, but the words to say so would not come. Instead she shrieked, "Woweee! We're going home! We're going home to Gramma and Grampa and Jerry and Dicky and all the family!" and she broke away to do a dizzy dance around the room.

Alan Frost and his wife exchanged understanding smiles. She did not need to tell them—they knew how she felt.

1084